PRAISE FOR *BRIGHTFELLOW*

"Ms. Ducornet's novel about a man who 'cannot fathom the bottomless secret of his own existence' casts a lingering spell." *—The New York Times*

"In tracing the shape of what is left behind, Ducornet lends dignity to the universal plight of vanished illusions." *—Los Angeles Times*

"Bursting with vivid imagery, beautiful language, heart-breaking characters . . . Ducornet's tale is unique and captivating." *—Booklist*

"A portrait of a surreal community that defies easy categorization. . . . An endless delight at the sentence level." *—Kirkus*

"Ducornet has written the oddest of varsity novels, one that anchors its charming caprice, philosophical fancy, and thriller-like pace to the psychological horror that lurks just beyond childhood innocence." *—Publishers Weekly*

PRAISE FOR RIKKI DUCORNET

"Ducornet is a novelist of ambition and scope."
—*The New York Times*

"Linguistically explosive. . . . One of the most interesting American writers around." —*The Nation*

"Pick up a book by the award-winning Ducornet, and you know it will be startling, elegant, and perfectly formed."
—*Library Journal*

"Storytelling that enchants the senses." —*The Boston Globe*

"Ducornet is a writer of extraordinary power, in whose books 'rigor and imagination' (her watchwords) perform with the grace and daring of high-wire acrobats." —*BOMB*

"Ducornet's is a world of surfaces so rich and textured that notions of meaning and interpretation are subsumed under a lush and seductive prose that eventually inhabits readers' minds." —*The Millions*

"Reveals strangeness in the most basic circumstances of life, flooding them in new light." —*Kenyon Review*

"Ducornet is a mad maestro of words." —*Seattle Weekly*

"Writer, poet, and artist Ducornet does things with words most authors would never even dream of." —*Men's Journal*

"Rikki Ducornet is a magic sensualist, a writer's writer, a master of language, a unique voice." —Amy Tan

"It is Rikki Ducornet's magic to be able to coax an entire universe—'restless beyond imagining, a universe of rock and flame, whose nature is incandescence'—out of the modest and often grim contours of one man's life." —Kathryn Davis

"*Netsuke* comes at the summit of Rikki Ducornet's passionate, caring, and accomplished career. Its readers will pick up pages of painful beauty and calamitous memory, and their focus will be like a burning glass; its examination of a ruinous sexual life is as delicate and sharp as a surgeon's knife. And the rendering? The rendering is as good as it gets."
—William Gass

"Rikki Ducornet can create an unsettling, dreamlike beauty out of any subject. In the heady mix of her fiction, everything becomes potently suggestive, resonant, fascinating. She exposes life's harshest truths with a mesmeric delicacy and holds her readers spellbound." —Joanna Scott

"Rikki Ducornet is imagination's emissary to this mundane world." —Stephen Sparks, Point Reyes Books

TRAFIK

OTHER NOVELS BY RIKKI DUCORNET

Brightfellow

Entering Fire

The Fan-Maker's Inquisition

The Fountains of Neptune

Gazelle

The Jade Cabinet

Netsuke

Phosphor in Dreamland

The Stain

TRAFIK

Rikki Ducornet

COFFEE HOUSE PRESS

Minneapolis

2021

Coffee House Press books are available to the trade through our primary distributor, Consortium Book Sales & Distribution, cbsd.com or (800) 283-3572. For personal orders, catalogs, or other information, write to info@coffeehousepress.org.

Coffee House Press is a nonprofit literary publishing house. Support from private foundations, corporate giving programs, government programs, and generous individuals helps make the publication of our books possible. We gratefully acknowledge their support in detail in the back of this book.

LIBRARY OF CONGRESS CATALOGING-IN-PUBLICATION DATA
Names: Ducornet, Rikki, 1943- author.
Title: Trafik / Rikki Ducornet.
Description: Minneapolis : Coffee House Press, 2021. | "A novel in
    warp drive."
Identifiers: LCCN 2020052682 | ISBN 9781566896061 (paperback) |
    ISBN 9781566896122 (ebook)
Subjects: GSAFD: Science fiction.
Classification: LCC PS3554.U279 T73 2021 | DDC 813/.54--dc23
LC record available at https://lccn.loc.gov/2020052682

ACKNOWLEDGEMENTS
Translated by Anne McLean, *From the Observatory* is published by Archipelago Books.
Just about everything Al Pacino says has been said by Christopher Walken. When credited to Christopher Walken, the voice is the author's.

PRINTED IN THE UNITED STATES OF AMERICA
28 27 26 25 24 23 22 21   1 2 3 4 5 6 7 8

For my son, Jean-Yves, and for Michael Lee, first readers.
Thank you, dear friends, for the precious hours
and the MUSIC!

But were mind immortal wont to
change its bodies, how topsy-turvy
earth's creatures!

—LUCRETIUS

TRAFIK

A NOVEL IN WARP DRIVE

CAKE AND CORTÁZAR

Sometimes Quiver feels so outside of everything, so peculiar, she catches herself scratching and poking her face in the manner of a caged monkey on the verge of insanity. She is doing this now, having left the Lights and making her way back to Home Free and Mic. As soon as he sees her, Mic offers her a slice of warm chocolate cake. Stove has baked it, but the icing is a molecular shuffle of his own inspiration. It has the *tonguefeel* (his word) of chocolate mousse—something she has never tasted.

Mic, having recently been introduced to the Kyoto App, is dressed like a geisha. Both of his lenticulars are punctuated with a dot. These, he explains, serve as a geisha's eyebrows. Gratefully, Quiver eats the cake and then slips off to shower and nap. Shower massages her in all the right places, but this is a shallow comfort. Once an avatar from another galaxy had—by no fault of its own—entered the shower at the very moment she had climaxed. Quiver's muffled cries were enough to send it packing. To her dismay, there was no way she could coax it back. Such encounters happened all too rarely, and this avatar was unusually charming. It reminded her of Julio Cortázar, who, before he died, had the face of a lion. Cortázar, who wrote: *The red headed night should see us walking with our face to the breeze.* Just what, she wonders, is a breeze?

THE LIGHTS

Always at the start of First Cycle and before getting down to things, Quiver runs in the woods with the Lights. This time, as she had specified, there is an owl in each tree. Owls and a brook full of fish—similar to those she had encountered on the walls of tombs when, as a child, she visited the Nile River Valley within the Lights.

This cycle, and for the first time, she glimpses a girl with dazzling red hair who, as she runs past, gazes into her eyes with a crazy and unforeseen intensity. It occurs to Quiver that the girl is associated with the owls, that if she asks for owls each time, she will likely see her again. And she does. The following First Cycle, the girl streaks past directly in the path, her hair ablaze in the interstices of the leaves, her sudden face as vivid as a comet. Quiver thinks that if they were together, the moments would always quicken like this. Later she tells Mic about the owls and the fish, but for now keeps the redhead to herself. Overhead the Plonk Sidereal Atlas sparks with stars. They are approaching the Small Magellanic Cloud.

For Mic, the Lights are all about cities. City streets, the souks brimming with things of hammered copper and brass in stacks. Boxes of tools, ruined ceiling fans, wire, wrenches, screwdrivers, and brass tacks. Manhattan. Its orange and yellow taxis. Their bright bumpers. Elevators. Hollywood. Above all: Hollywood. When Quiver sleeps, he roams the Chateau Marmont. Lounges poolside. Becomes intimate with coffee makers, the showerheads, and majestic freezers. Mic adores the Chateau Marmont. And Al Pacino. His sprawling pad, its many faucets. Pacino's faucets! His blender, his juicer!

ALONE WITH MIC

It was in space, alone with Mic, that Quiver came to fully appreciate her vanished lover, who, if vitalized and enhanced, was, as was she, nonetheless categorized as terrestrial. Her lover was the one who stood out among all the others—those who were memorable, who had taken form within a mother's womb. She thinks of her lover's immaculate feet, naked as fish, the fish she had seen in the Lights. Back in Home Free with Mic once again, she is longing for her lover and for her own self concurrently, the self she was in her lover's proximity, her embrace.

Quiver is a transitional prototype. She had gestated in a dynamic carbon envelope that, suspended from a rack, swelled as she swelled, her umbilical cord fused to a vitamin sack. Row after row, the envelopes and the sacks hung in the air. It was said that they were festive—music for the eyes. She hates to think of it.

Transitionals such as Quiver were fraught, an irritable bunch at best. Which is why she travels with Mic. Mic is good in emergencies, as when she *flips her fuses* (his words). Always on the lookout, and at the end of Second Cycle, he downloads her dreams. Although rooted in simulations and threadbare memories, Quiver's dreams are authentically hers. Mic keeps a careful record, and in this way knows when she is close to flipping. Mic, too, is volatile. And when he *comes apart at the seams* (her words), Quiver weighs in. It is in this way that they are considered right for one another.

To be clear, it must be said that both are most capable. Both had been trained for rare mineral reconnaissance and extraction, and to interact graciously in limited environments.

Mic has something of an old-world sensibility—likely due to his passion for terrestrial cinema, popular music, and, most recently, all things Japanese—a sensibility that Quiver finds precious. This Mic had picked up at once, yet what can he do? His Swift Wheel is packed with music and movies! These are what keep Mic motivated and happy. But in her worst moments, Quiver fears he had been hardwired to aggravate her. She fears they had been teamed up so that he could observe and document her descent into madness— always a possibility for even the most muscled prototypes.

Mic is well aware of her sensitivities and at his best understands and respects her ongoing need to turn to the Lights for solace. Her need to run in the woods, on the mountain trails and country roads of vanished places. He, too, is wired to so much that is (or had been) terrestrial. In this way they share a profound (and most likely essential) experience of the original planet.

THE KYOTO APP

Mic is short for Michelangelo (and not microphone—although a thumbnail-sized microphone is emblazoned on his minus end). When he stands at attention, his Swift Wheel humming, the display fume suspended before him, he percolates his way into whatever is going on. As when he wanders the souk of Aleppo, circa 1953, a discreet stowaway on a clueless couple's honeymoon. Or transits to Vienna that same year. (He likes the fifties, the pressure cookers, toasters, Waring Blenders, Studebakers—that sexy front end!) He searches a wealth of material on Studebakers and succumbs to an ongoing and helpless crush, unable to speak of anything else until Quiver threatens him with a vinegar bath—vinegar one of Mic's vulnerabilities ever since he had come close to perishing on a previous mission during a freak encounter with oscillating plasma clouds gorged with vinegar. They had returned to Elsewhere at once where he was polished within an inch of his life. When it was over, Quiver touched what stood for his shoulder with something like tenderness. His voice breaking, Mic had thanked her for what he called *comforting me in a human way.* Sometime later he had reached out to her similarly, patting her shoulder with that adaptable hand of his, eight fingers that could in a quik become a claw, a hammer, a rake, a set of tweezers, a bottle opener. The gesture was unforeseen. Quiver had shuddered so violently that Mic, looking into her eyes with those ever-shifting lenticulars of his—now green, now orange, now red—shed what was apparently a tear. Later she saw the tear gleaming on the floor beneath Food Face. Picking it up, she was surprised to see a small marble of cat's-eye Jasper—the very thing the children of the Home Planet had prized in their games of bum-hole. Mic's tear was the first and only marble Quiver would ever see. She kept it for a "rainy day": a thing she knew but virtually, she kept it for "luck."

The Kyoto App provides musical entertainment. Mic excels at clappers, gongs, flute, and drum; strings. As she nibbles her Newton Bar and sips her gigahertz mixer, he offers up a haunting melody. It conjures everything the Lights have taught her about the terrestrial night, tree frogs, and spring weather. As the music recedes, Mic recites from the *Makura no Soshi:*

> *It is night. Expecting a visitor, one is*
> *startled by the sounds of rain striking*
> *the shutters.*

Thrust into agitation, Quiver sighs, sobs, shouts out, and—*loses it.* When she comes to, she is strapped into her hamok and must wheedle and cajole before Micosan agrees to her unbuckling. After, to make peace, he offers her a Francis Crick and a fragrant tea served in a replica raku tea bowl. The tea is soothing, and the Crick her favorite cracker. As she snacks, Mic screens her dream:

She is swimming in the ocean of an unknown planet's atmosphere. She is a fish, a small orange carp, swimming among other fish—all mirrors of herself. Looking closely, she sees they are each fused in ice or, perhaps, glass. She, too, is immobilized within the glass, possibly immortal, in any case unreachable. Now she is somehow herself, Quiver, running down a garden path toward a charming building in a sea of sound: tree frogs, crickets, birds. Something unprecedented is about to happen.

The screen idle now, Quiver looks away and sees that Mic—in red pants and a red jacket with gold epaulettes—has taken on the colors and demeanor from another time entirely. A red pillbox hat is poised on what serves as his head, and his flashing lenticulars convey pleasure in what is clearly the outcome of a carefully considered determination. He proposes a deal. If she says nothing about this, he will not inform Elsewhere about her recurrent breakdowns.

"But, don't they see it all?" Quiver asks. "I thought—"

"For some time now," he tells her, "Base sees nothing but a scramble of statik."

"Wow! But, Mic! What *are* you?"

"A bellhop! A bell would ring and he, looking divine, would *hop to it*! Just like a bot!" He executes a series of near somersaults in place, filling Home Free with the sounds of bells of all kinds, sounds she had never before heard: kitchen oven timers, egg timers, alarm clocks, dinner bells, cowbells, church chimes, horse-and-buggy bells, elephant and goat bells, cat bells—until she shouts "LAY OFF MIC!"— only to be outdone by the Plonk Sidereal Atlas, its voice rising above hers, if somewhat incoherently announcing that they are closing in on Quasi. *Closeting Quasi!* it rumbles: *Closeting!*

In this way, on they go together, Micosan and Quiver, deeper into the incomprehending night, deftly avoiding a sudden sea of leaking protons and always into the ineffable future.

FUMEVAP

A new cycle begins. Here she is, once again, grappling with a malfunctioning fumevap. The task is hers, because the fumes—such as they are (a discreet fart now and then, for forking sake!)—are *hers*. It is rare that Mic's pankwizer scorches, you see, and even when it does, its funk is nearly imperceptible. Periodically, however, Mic tumbles into a radical metaphysical mood, his botsplaining accumulating exponentially. He will say:

"A bot never passes fumes!"

He will say: "You cannot fix your own forking fumevap!"

It is true that the fumevap often refuses to cooperate. But from farts to fumevaps, Mic leaps to diesel engines, factory chimneys, the bombing of the souk in Aleppo, the demise of movie palaces—and this thanks to a TRAGICALLY FLAWED DIGESTIVE APPARATUS COMPROMISED BY MELANCHOLY, UNFULFILLED ASPIRATIONS, AT THE MERCY OF ALLERGENS, BACTERIAL INFECTIONS, FOOD POISONING, PARASITES, FAILING TEETH, THE RIDICULOUS STOMACH, UNTRUSTWORTHY GALL BLADDER, OUTRAGEOUS RECTUM, AND THE PESKY ESOPHAGUS!

Quiver rallies and, crossing the room, confronts Mic with her height, majestic on legs that, to Mic's dismay, *go on forever.*

"You forking self-righteous GIZMO!" she shrieks. "The normal functioning of my body is not an indignity! It is not a misdemeanor! You are accusing me of being human—you maddening THINGAMABOB! And even if it is true that I am incapable of photosynthesis and cannot go solar, still . . . I mean . . . you, too, Mic, will succumb to space-time sooner or later! You, too, are subject to change! Subject to endings! TO ENDINGS, MIC!"

CONTACTS TO MOLECULAR

Mic is so distraught by Quiver's outburst he suffers a brief glottological rust rash. For the first time in their history together, he is deprived of speech. His back pressed up against the ice machine, he stares into the void Quiver has just now revealed to him. Never before has he "felt" so existentially compromised. He ponders Quiver's significant otherness. Never before has she described him so disparagingly! Never before has he been made to consider his own finitude!

Quiver, also visibly shaken, gazes at Mic with concern. She reminds herself that Mic was conceived to serve in human domestic realms as much as with machines and the vexing realms—above all unknown—that they must navigate together. He once called their relationship "an entanglement"—which at the time enraged her. But now she thinks he is right. It *is* an entanglement—an entanglement within myriad entanglements behind, ahead, and all around them.

Mic, she considers, is after all a deeply thoughtful gizmo. He had been wired to think, to brood, to philosophize, to solve complex problems, to—lest she forget—keep her from cracking. What's more, the galley heat transporter and condensed matter coolers had both disfunctioned at the very same moment she had *lost it* and shouted at him, reminding her that Mic is connected to every single one of the gizmos on board.

"Micosan," she murmurs, walking to him, tenderly reaching out to him, gently caressing his insulator topper. "It's o.k., baby. I am well aware," she continues. "I am grateful that each and every nanoparticle in this Wobble depends on you. There is no statistical evaluation, not a single bias sweep, not one inquiry into spectors, scales, or peaks that happens without you. And yet, despite these never-ending tasks, *you keep on trucking,* every quik *you are here—*thoughtfully, Mic, attentively in the present. Thanks to you, we *soar,* baby! And always at a perfectly maintained room temperature, no matter the challenges. No matter how very, very cold, how very, very hot!" Then, knowing how much he loves to hear a human sing a song just about more than anything, she sings one of Phys Chem's greatest hits: *Contacts to Molecular,* which begins (as surely you recall):

> *I wanna monitor*
> *your interferometer*
> *contact molecular*
> *exaltor homuncular*
> *wanna accelerate*
> *your scintillator*
> *your scintillator*
> *wanna check out*
> *your interstellar laser*
> *titillate your laser!*

ON BEING

The following First Cycle, Mic confronts Quiver as soon as she unfolds from her hamok and even before she hits the floor.

"I am a *self*!" Mic, beyond excited, levitates from within a diaphanous halo of steam.

"Yes! Yes! I know, Mic! I—"

"Not so fast!" Mic cries, his voice rising as he orbits the breakfast table, a trail of mist behind him. "You see, I have been mulling this over in the dark, an interminable darkness so dark even the Space Eye was empty of light."

"O.K.! O.K.! I get it, and—"

"Here it is!" Mic cries. "Are you listening, Quiv?"

"I am! I am!"

"I am a self *because I think*!"

"Yes! Yes! I *get it*—"

"Quiet, Quiv! There is more! *So much more!* If I am because I think, this means I *am thought*!"

"Wow, baby. I guess so—"

"Quiver! This means that I AM NOT A GIZMO!" Satisfied, he rolls off, eager to consider the current cycle's itinerary. Thoughtful, Quiver nibbles her Crick. *I have been soulblind,* she thinks, overwhelmed by self-loathing.

QUASI

Inexorably, First Cycle returns. A small company of owls as soft as moths rise from the forest canopy and scatter. Her hair beating the air like a wing, the redhead dashes past, within a breath dissolving. Such encounters remind Quiver that she has rarely known such moments of release. Of expectation.

The few steps she takes from the Lights to Home Free are taken in absolute solitude. But now she sees Mic, the Space Eye, and Quasi rise above them, one rock among many and not much larger than the rest. A red star—named Melodious (the Atlas informs them)—blinks in a corner.

Toggling closer they see spars of multiple Fibonacci flowerets the color of ham, each as tall as the Burj Khalifa before it was swamped by the sea. "Quasi's silicate skeleton and barbed electromagnetic spuds are constructed much like my thought box," Mic says. "Already I feel an affinity. This is propitious. Destiny, perhaps."

"You were," Quiver advises him acidly, "conceived and constructed for the very purpose of mineral extraction. It is no accident we have been sent to Quasi."

"I was *constructed,* yes! As you say! No need to remind me of *that.* Unlike you, *you* who are the outcome of a cascade of random and chronic accidents! Whereas I—let us not forget it—I am the outcome of a *precise cause.*"

"As was I, you, you . . . botling! I hung suspended in the nursery *for a purpose*! And by the way! You look like a bottle of hot sauce in that outfit," she scolds, unable to contain herself.

"That nursery reeked like the dead oceans of First World!" is his reply. "Or so I suppose, as one forced to ambulate in your proximity, cycle after cycle, in a space not much larger than a shoe closet—a *small* shoe closet," Mic adds as an afterthought. (His was one of the rare intelligences for whom such things mattered. He had been impressed by the opulence of Paris Hilton's own shoe closet as seen on the Swift Wheel's Celebrating Celebrities' Closets App.)

"How?" she wonders. "How can you go on (as is your wont) about my supposed off-gassing when you, Mic—I hate to tell you this—*have no nose,* but only an orifice not much bigger than a keyhole in a door, a bunghole of a—"

"Now you *sound like me!*" Mic yelps, bouncing up and down like a toddler in a tantrum.

"Not at all!" Quiver thunders above him. "It is you, *you,* you counterfeit, you accumulation of soup cans, you interloper—who has been wired *to sound like me!*"

"Not so!" Mic, still bouncing, rages, his lenticulars rattling like dice in what passes for his head. "Not so! You thing of cosmical irreverence! I am the voice of the imminent present! IT IS SILICA THAT WINS THE BATTLE! IT IS GRAPHITE THAT SOLVES THE MYSTERY! IT IS THE MAGNET AT MY CORE THAT HAS THE LAST WORD! Wait and see!" In his excitement his pillbox hat begins to levitate. It circles the room, stalls, charges, and under full steam lunges for her. She grabs her ever-handy sonic dust-ionizing defibulator and strikes as Mic attempts to duck. The hat explodes with a pop as, concurrently, Mic's frustulator sheds a silver trickle of electromagnetic gravy.

"Ah! Mic!" Quiver approaches him, concerned. He grabs her by a strap; they fall to the floor and grapple like primates. Sobbing marbles he says: "Don't you ever mess with my frustulator!"

"I aimed at the forking *hat*!" Quiver says as the hat's scattered particles attempt to regroup and instead collide with marbles. The absurdity of everything catches up with her and she finds herself helplessly laughing.

"You need me, Mic!" she sputters between gales of laughter. "Without me who will lubricate your poke hole? Who will . . . will stimulate your . . . alt, alterior . . . thermonics?"

"Your species is damned," he says softly, seemingly exhausted. And then, as an afterthought: "Everything is doomed. But for the light! THE LIGHT!" Exulted, he spins on his axle in a kind of joyful trance. He is recalling his prototype, dear little Radio 1 (Rad for short), who would spin for the pleasure of it, his one little amethyst lenticular focused on the sun. (A memory that goes way back, when from the Moon it was still possible to see the sun and, beneath its beneficial influence, be flooded with joy.) "I am thinking now of little Rad," he explains, as if nothing had happened and they were starting the First Cycle all over again.

Quiver is touched that a bot and a boy of Silica and Fluorescent Graphite with sparse electron density had once gazed at the sun with pleasure—something she herself recalls with longing. And Mic, pleased that Quiver is looking at him with tenderness, says: "I am your friend, Quiv. Even though you ignite my fuses. Even if you will always be . . . strange!"

These words are punctuated by a thud and a blistering landing on Quasi. (In their rage they had completely forgotten that they were about to arrive at destination!) Brutally rocked back and forth, they cling to Food Face as the Plonk Sidereal Atlas upbraids them repeatedly until things settle down and they can prod its pin: *Screwup! Screwup! Screwup! Topographical Error!*

They are perilously perched on a spiraling outcropping of spars a great distance from Rucker's Parameter—the one place on Quasi that is flat and in proximity to APM: the area of potential mines.

"I started that quarrel," Mic says gloomily, once they are steady. "And this despite everything the Kyoto App has taught me about civility. I am ashamed. I bow before you, Quiv." Then he does.

EMU PARK

Stuck on a spar, they have no choice but to call upon the benzine escalator, a tricky vehicle salvaged from a disenfranchised Pico Cycle (as an afterthought), and stashed in cargo. That the Pico Cycle had been dumped on them was just another example of how they have been treated all along. And why? Wasn't Quasi's mineral wealth enough to ensure the project's importance? Hadn't Quiver proved her own worth having been one of the first to orbit Saturn, spending 730 cycles riding the ether among the fricative flotsam in a solar wind that whistled and trilled so incessantly that she suffers tinnitus even now, yet has never once complained? Hadn't Mic withstood the terrible rages of Jupiter's storm clouds, accumulating data on over twelve thousand unknown particulates, including the supermarvelous nonionizing Cuticular Sidebar? The very sidebar that is now the required first integument for absolutely all Deep Space vehicular traffic?

The neglect is stupefying. And now, here they are, down in cargo, tugging at the forking benzine escalator, pushing and prodding it into position in the nook at the back of dexter hatch, cussing. Once entombed, dressed in their sidebar haulovers and boots, they are violently thrust, up and away, leaving their pod unsteadily poised—they can see just how unsteadily—on the rim of that ridiculous maze of spars that, in Mic's words, are of an unprecedented hue, an *obscene pinkitude*—as if the guts of a gigantic mole rat had been torn out, spliced, and left standing to freeze dry on top of a sponge the size of Manhattan (that is to say, before Washout, Noise, and that city's consequent collapse). She agrees that the terrain is horrible and unlike anything they have encountered. But just then, as they shriek, the Wobble, having been unbalanced by the escalator's explosive ejection, topples over and, on a roll, careens down the spar's slick edge only to vanish.

"I cannot," says Quiver, the cinnamon of her face now pallid, "I cannot, cannot—"

Mic, recalling that he is wired to be indefatigably serviceable, and in the mellow tones of his favorite homeboy psychobot, says: "We will do what we were sent to do. We will redeploy the benzine escalator, prepare for excavating, find the Wobble, load cargo, and return to Elsewhere with Harvey Troano and what looks like vast accumulations of nonionizing Cuticular in proton-bunch populations, glowing—see that to the dexter?—like cobs of gold teeth!"

"Forking unbelievable!" Quiver exclaims, and then she screams. The ground at their feet is glistering with the bioluminescent spores of the fantastically omnivorous bacillus-grumpus-eptaxis. It spreads in all directions like wildfire. In the heat of the moment, they had neglected to sterilize their boots, infecting the Quasian terrain and precipitating a catastrophic mutation that will in no time cause the spongeous asteroid to shrink, to splinter into one vast Cuticular Sidebar cracker.

Without delay and with the help of their profiterole lasers and rooter blades, they tear into the highly prized material, slice it into irregular squares friable as salteens, stuff it into the escalator, speed across a worsening pattern of fissures in the direction they had last seen the Wobble, and discover that it has landed on its side but with the escalator's elevator *face up*! It takes a number of jacks, ladders, pulleys, and complaints to get the escalator and its precious cargo back into the elevator, but in time it is done and they are able to, exhausted, clamber inside the Wobble and Home Free, where at once Quiver tumbles into her hamok, and Mic, decompressing his vesticular corridor, indulges in a refreshing barometric foaming. Then, as Quiver slumbers, wading into a deep dream in which the redhead approaches her, time after time, to gently caress her cheek with tender curiosity, Mic informs their base commander, Alpha Astron, that they are returning with a full cargo. Alpha Astron appears at once, looming on the ceiling, barking: "Sidebar? Sidebar?"

"Sidebar!" Mic crows, despite a surge of misgiving deep within his central coil. Satisfied, Alpha Astron vanishes in a puddle of ink.

To ease his anxiety, Mic dives into his latest fascination—an antique terrestrial game: Emu Park. It takes place in the Anza-Borrego Desert decades before the cascading events that erased First Planet and, soon after, the Moon.

Mic is crazy for the emus. They are *chibi*—meaning irresistibly cute—a cross between a bird and a camel. In the game, the emus and the roadrunner are the central characters. Mic sides with the emus every time, acquires a number of Chaldean trailers and dozens of truckloads of unexamined junk that he parks beside the Salton Sea.

There are treasures to be found in the trailers and the trucks such as a Carthaginian compass that will direct his number-one emu to a secret river in space that leads to the Light and Sidereal Survival. (The loser is tossed into a galaxy of dubious origins and is banished to a sublunar purgatory in an undiscoverable dimension.) There are celestial mountains of marvelous metals to be found. There are schools of comets whose entrails illuminate the pathways to seers and mediums. There are sinkholes to universes made of coral, of beeswax, of feathers and scales. There is always the risk of collision, of dissolution, of implosion, explosion, of never-ending solitude, of irritating the gods, of being snapped up by hungry ghosts—the ghosts of those whose destinies have been torn from them. There is always the promise of reaching an ocean of light foaming with delights, generous with answers. Ah! How Mic loves Emu Park!

Later, when Quiver awakens from her nap, Mic, radiating in a gold lamé kimono, serves her centrifuged rice and squid simulate. Eager to check out cargo and itemize what they had managed to salvage, Quiver bolts her food. A good supply of sidebar and Harvey Troano will make up for other losses, perhaps stave off any investigations. But when they descend into cargo's vacuum chamber, they find only a fine dust that, suspended further, dissolves as they look. Scrambling back to Home Free, they frantically search for Quasi on the Plonk Sidereal Atlas. Although the Atlas bleeps with bodies bright and dark, large and small—Quasi is undetectable.

"Where?" Mic dares ask the Atlas. "Where is Quasi?"

Encroached, the Atlas intones lugubriously. *Encroached, Infected, and Eliminated. And Eliminated. And Eliminated.*

"Forking unbelievable!" Quiver cries. "We're cooked."

GOING ROGUE

The moment is momentous. They will have to report back to Elsewhere, admit their phenomenal negligence, suffer raised eyebrows, stagnate in Limbo as Alpha Astron decides their next—and it will be dangerous and humiliating—assignment.

"That is," Quiver whispers, "unless we go rogue." They are standing inside the kombucha cooler with the door closed. The cooler is calming. "I've never acquired a taste for kombucha," says Quiver, "yet here we are." They feel the Wobble slowly rolling in place, listen to the familiar sound of kombucha sloshing in its vat. "I've often wondered what was making that noise," says Quiver. "I feared it was happening in my mind."

"If we go rogue," says Mic, "let's go to Trafik."

"Trafik!" Quiver approves.

They abandon the cooler and, standing beneath the Space Eye, gaze up at the swarming stars.

"The attention of the cosmos is focused upon us," she says. "Their blinking is the way they signal to one another and to us."

Disencumbered by all expectations and restraints, the sequencer flashes azure, a black hole claims its center, and Bugs Bunny appears wearing a top hat.

"Eeh!" he says. "What's up, Doc?"

"Trafik," says Mic.

"Trafik!" says Bugs. "Coming right up!"

"What was *that*?" Quiver asks dumbfounded.

"Hollywood," says Mic. "An avatar of yore."

Later, as Quiver eats her freeze-dried sashimi, Mic recalls how they had, not so very long ago, mined the terrestrial ring together, those radical density lumps of wrought iron, Jurassic sandstone (much of it having originated in Brooklyn), architectural glass, paving stones, gravel, highway tar, powder room ceramics, and so on—all this having been thrust into orbit the instant Noise blasted, taking with it solar cells, satellites, and the stuff of falling stars. This trash had so mightily incrassated, it was near impossible to break apart. A toxic hard candy, it stuck to, abraded, and fractured the stoutest extirpators, clotburs, and hanks. Sometimes the mass came unbound unexpectedly and sent them careening into the abrasive faces of oscillating unclumped variables—all of them ejecting unprecedented gasses.

From the start, Mic had declaimed: "We won't last a day." After what seemed like forever he said: "We're not doing it." And Quiver agreed. Even then they were on the verge of going rogue.

"If only we had the adequate vehicle!" she had said at the time. "We could go off to Barometer Miles and find ourselves a cozy chrome yurt. We could go to . . . Trafik!" It was at that very moment when they had *had it,* that Base dropped the project. Sent them off to mine asteroids. A thing they had done diligently, if with uneven success.

SURFING THE ENDOCYCLIC QUASAR MASS

They are surfing the Endocyclic Quasar Mass. Mic chirps into service and rolls over to Food Face. He sees a dog—he knows it is a dog. He has seen the stars walking their dogs on Zircon-studded leashes. This dog is looking wistfully out the galley Space Eye. A dog of "medium size," he reports to Quiver as he hands her a foaming neuropeptide smoothie. "Spotted in the manner of a Holstein-Friesian, some sort of fire truck dog."

"But, just what is a Holstein-Friesian?" Quiver wants to know.

"A cow once eaten in such quantity, the terrestrial atmosphere *went brillig*—an old-timey word coined when grilling and broiling ruled culinary culture."

"And what is it, then, to broil and grill?" Quiver asks, still only half awake.

"The flesh was seared," Mic reports, "beneath or upon flames."

"Flames in the galley?" Quiver ponders, yawning. "Why? Why when Food Face will do the cooking cold?"

"There was no Food Face then," says Mic, deep into his investigations. "Oh! And listen to this! When Hydrant 3 landed on Titan and proclaimed, *Tis brillig,* he was referring to the density of the atmosphere and the mood of the moment. Earth's atmosphere was like that near the end."

The dog unglues from the galley Space Eye, turns, and lopes toward them, whimpering.

"What can it possibly want?" asks Quiver.

"We are multitudes," the dog tells her in a voice at once a rasp and a groan. "I am but the first to hatch."

"Dogs do not hatch!" Mic says with conviction. "My Swift Wheel states this clearly!" He sees a bit of trash on the floor and, always fastidious, picks it up and tosses it at Sweep. A pod of some sort, or cocoon.

"Hmm," mutters Quiver, now awake. "Something's going on." A quik later, a second dog appears, exactly like the first. It, too, gazes out of the galley Space Eye wistfully. In another quik or two, three more dogs manifest, all pressing against one another in their attempt to look out the Space Eye. The floor is now littered with pods, and the galley Space Eye is hidden behind a crush of medium-sized Holstein-Friesian spotted fire truck dogs.

"Bloody delirious!" Quiver howls. "We need an immediate ID on clonal tags NOW!"

"Got it," cries Mic. "I've deployed reprogramming trajectories!"

Quiver dashes about Home Free looking into every corner to locate the stowaway pods—none larger than a pineal gland. Erect and flashing, having charged the specific antagonistic receptor magnet, Sweep is up to the task, nabbing pods in the laundry, in the optical pantry, clumped like grapes in corners and hanging like bats from the fume-vap. Instigating a temporary quark well above a speedily contrived and fatal attractor, the pods are sucked up and sent tumbling to another dimension entirely. However, the hatched dogs remain, pressed together and gazing into space, whimpering and whining mournfully.

"Is there somewhere you want to go?" Quiver asks them, gently caressing their furry shoulders.

"Dolly's Dream Dog B and B in Tuscaloosa!" they whine together, their complaints rising and falling like the wind.

"Tuscaloosa, Alabama?" Mic asks. The dogs all begin to yap excitedly: *yes! YES!*

"But surely! You must know! Earth is gone! It's *gone*! It's been gone for generations!" Quiver cries out. "GONE! Forking unbelievable!"

The dogs' moans fill the Wobble with what can only be described as a brillig mood. They are now pressing together with such conviction she shouts at them to stop, afraid they will smother themselves. But the dogs ignore her and continue to muscle against each other, pushing and shoving with such force they coalesce into one vast indissoluble animal—a magnificent Holstein-Friesian cow. "Just look at the caliber of its tailward breach!" Mic shrieks.

The cow begins to groan. Or is it, Quiv wonders, a bleating? A whinnying? A gabbling?

"It must be a mooing," Mic reports, "for mooing is the sound a cow makes." (In all her time spent in the Lights, Quiver has not once met up with a cow.)

"Well," says Quiver. "Here we are. I have no idea how to solve this, Mic, and I am going to take a nap." As soon as she tucks into her hamok, the cow further coalesces, condenses, recedes, and wanes. All that remains is a black spot on the floor.

QUIVER DREAMS OF ALFA ASTRON

Quiver dreams of Alpha Astron. He dervishes into her dream exploding with rage. Quasi! he screams. Quasi! He has a large black tattoo on his neck shaped like an egg. Compact and immobile, it is imponderable, sinister, and menacing. Alfa Astron, she thinks, is an archon. He has kept his identity hidden beneath his impressive collection of turtleneck sweaters. In Quiver's dream, Alpha Astron's closet opens its portals, its interior unspooling like the hallways on the Moon. A closet like the ones Mic studies so closely, closets having once belonged to Hollywood stars, crammed with tangibles, disguises and stuff, suspended in time and space within a perpetual blizzard of dust. These, when retrieved, transform the body into something transcendent. Alpha Astron's body, for example, whose influence extends so far beyond the home galaxy it is uncanny, even for those for whom the uncanny is the road most traveled.

In Quiver's dream, Alpha Astron's shalloon turtlenecks, his sharkskin loungers, his spider-silk dickeys and cravats, and his tooled boots and spats are stacked up like mineral deposits in a quarry beyond the sun's reach. In order to get dressed, Alpha Astron needs the intervention of radio and x-ray emissions. Except for his sock drawer. The sock drawer has its own moon. The sock drawer's contents have been bathing in moonlight for so long, they are sopping with afterglow. Quiver recognizes some of her own socks long ago missing.

Still dreaming, Quiver looks up into the Plonk Sidereal Atlas and sees that Alpha Astron's egg-shaped tattoo has migrated to the glass. Stuck on the outside, it is impossible to remove, considering the risks of entering into the Counter Punctual Velocity Bubble's plasmic spume. Yet it glowers at the center of the Atlas Space Eye, obstructing all that lies ahead.

As soon as Quiver awakens, she leaps from her hamok and tells Mic to download her dream. As soon as he sees it, he tells her to return to her hamok at once with a mental image of a wire sponge. She is to return to her dream and scrub Alpha Astron's egg tattoo off the outer face of the Plonk Sidereal Atlas.

As soon as she hits the hamok, Quiver falls asleep and begins to dream. In her dream she suits up and exits the Wobble, dives into the Counter Punctual Velocity Bubble's plasma spume, swims to the Plonk Sidereal Atlas Space Eye, sees the tattoo's black egg stuck to the glass. The Bubble's plasma is like a cool, loose jello that, as she approaches the egg, gets warmer and warmer and begins to thicken. The heat rises as does a noise emanating from the egg itself, roaring like a trillion vintage vacuum cleaners. Quiver scrubs the surface until it gives, opening like a mouth. She shoves the wire sponge down the egg's throat where it is swallowed at once. Quiver looks on as the egg ogres itself, swallowing not only the wire sponge but its own absence until nothing remains but a spot no bigger than the eye of an ant. In a quik that, too, vanishes, reinstating harmonic order.

Meanwhile, Mic has been *on it*, targeting the major circuits and simultaneously enforcing a universal putative inhibition. He reconfigures the full array of rehabilitation paradigms. He has flooded the system with an instantaneous ice bath of field-induced saturable Graphene. The Atlas shudders, appears to crystalize, reaffirms transparency. Resurfacing from her dream and yawning, Quiver hears the voice of a diva from the distant past: FKA twigs singing: *Water Me.*

ONE MIGHT DO WELL TO MENTION THAT

Having banished Alpha Astron and in a celebratory mood, Mic, having served Quiver a second breakfast, offers up a kaleidoscopic terrestrial fashion show beginning with a stunning Saharan Berber astride a tasselated camel, moving on to Iggy Pop wearing nothing but a scarlet umbrella, Rihanna in salted almonds at the MET, Cardi B at the Latin Grammys, and ending with RuPaul. Quiver has never been so aware of the staggering extent of Mic's infinite holdings. Awestruck, she looks on with renewed admiration as he now rehearses his navigational skills, flashing shipping charts of the China Sea, the rail routes of India, the temples of Uxmal, the ancient highlands that once bounded the plain of Babylonia on its eastern side, a map of the streets of Asshur. With something like reverence, he retrieves an image of an expired Egyptian lake named Timsah: "the lake of crocodiles." Next they visit two Australian caves on a place once called Chasm Island in the Gulf of Carpentaria. She sees porpoises, turtles, kangaroos, and a human hand painted in red and black on the cave walls.

Mic begins to seriously overheat. His Swift Wheel, on the verge of scorched, is sent spinning at such velocity that even if they are not aware of it (at least not initially) and think there is simply a problem with Walpole's reverberator, they are now in another galaxy entirely. This is signified by the loud beeping and flashing of the resonator as it attempts to determine a known or familiar (or, at least, applicable) resonance frequency within the sudden exotic configuration. But this leads to further incoherence as somehow Nicki Minaj shows up in the mix singing *Starships.* On top of all this, due to a dysplastic tear, they are startled nearly out of their wits by a thoroughly unpleasant tenquid shuffle causing their atoms to discompose (if but for a quik in time), which reduces them to a fluid extracellular hyperpromiscuity (cellular decoherence)—in other words their latitudinal diversity gradients are smacked. (They are briefly reduced to soup.) In Quiver's words: "Wow! Alpha Astron will never find us now!"

Needless to say they recover, although Quiver suffers an intense inflammatory response to twerking for several cycles after, and Mic's own photoplethysmography systems now have a tendency to overcram—not that this really matters.

BETWEEN

How often, Quiver thinks, how often have I been without access to safety. How terrible it is and yet how familiar, to be forever on the verge of falling. And would it have been any different had I gestated in a womb and not in an envelope suspended in a darkened room, rocked by the breathing of a fumevap, the whispers of apprentices moving among us in their blues like ghosts? Sometimes I wonder if my excursions into space are not simply an excuse for leaping off a cliff.

How often have I been between planets, between worlds, between galaxies—without footing, relentlessly alone, without promise of release, trapped in the web of unknowing, the unending memory of loss.

Snailed (Mic's word) in her hamok, Quiver attempts to become as fluid as water. She has read that if she *becomes water* she will stop *feeling thirsty.* But where has Quiver read this, living as she has from the start in worlds without books? And what is this she holds against her heart, this person, Quiver, who still manages somehow to be a person although so much has been stolen right out from under her? As you have likely guessed, it is a book she holds, a beautiful book, its cover a gray jade, its title printed in lavender. A book by Julio Cortázar who wrote: *Terrible things can happen to us.* Who wrote: *The revolution is a sea of wheat.* A book that is a *transgression.* A book that had survived The Scouring and, having passed from hand to hand, reached her lover. On the verge of being disappeared, her lover had managed to assure that Quiver could find it. She had proposed a time and place for them to meet in one of the Moon's many hallways. Quiver recalls how an icy chill had moved through her. How the hall was empty, its air nearly exhausted. She thinks she will always be in this hallway, its blind doors and filthy windows of bubbled glass. She searches for signs. She comes upon the book, hidden beneath a bench. With a single gesture, takes it up, slips it beneath her shirt, sits down as if fatigued, looks at her feet, stretches and yawns and returns to her room.

Time passes. And then she finds the courage to open the book. Although the text is brief, never has she seen anything so extensive. Alone in the deep silence she takes the first page between her fingers, gently turning it over. She begins to read:

This way of being between, not above or behind but between, this orifice hour . . .

ONCE MORE MIC REFLECTS ON BEING MIC

Quiver's lover had been made to disappear. What does this mean, exactly? Alone in his corner beside the humming ice maker, Mic attempts to get a handle on such losses as in her hamok Quiver deeply sleeps. He thinks if he were more "instinctive" he might understand Quiver better.

Pensive, he considers his own detained erotic life, bewildered as always by his place in the physical world—a *man of tin* as, unforgettably, he had once been called to his face. A man born of an abstraction, contrived, schematized, then . . . *printed. Printed in parts!* Yet, he is, to use Quiver's words, a thing of *brute matter,* an embodied abstraction of human thought, a complex whole gifted with a context and an identity. If he is not "human," still, he *is human* in so many ways! *See how I suffer!* he thinks. *Is this not human? This suffering?*

And was Quiv's fascination for the virtual redhead any different from his own fascination with Al Pacino and his marvelous realms, his talismanic gizmos? His toaster! His blender! And if Al's faucets and the bellhop's buttons caused his central circuitry to spark—was this his fault? Had he not been programmed to receive, retain, and respond to the erratic, mutable, irresistible weather of human affectivity? Is he not, when gazing at Al's incomparable face, *uplifted*? Do not faces, toasters, brass buttons *give off light*? Is he not—as are so many living creatures—polyamorous? He thinks that if there is a word that describes him, he is not alone in the ways he lives.

For the first time in a very long while, he recalls his first encounter with a terrestrial music called *the blues.* He discovered that he was wired to something so much deeper than he had known possible; he reverberated to a voice as pure as the voice of a child, a bird, the wind. A voice that descended into the deepest waters, a *sexed* voice! Yes! This is what it must have been! That elusive weather, the sexed voice, repeating over and over again, *Come to me.* And Mic had wanted, more than he had ever wanted anything, to go to him, whoever he was, this "guy" whose heart was in sync with his own core receptor coil. Mic imagined the singer was a guy in a suit, like the guys in what was once called the movies; a guy not all that young, yet loose and tight all at the same time, leaning nonchalantly against a streetlight on the back wall of some mysterious establishment, such as a "bar," a "speakeasy"—some sort of personal amulet, a *chibi* chimney stack, gracefully held between his lips, lost in "reflection," lost in "love." At ease and intact in his own integument, in a way Mic could never quite comprehend. The guy is handsome—this Mic knew—but how? And why? This dreamy guy was a movie star, something Mic fully appreciated when he first fell in love (!) with the movies, fell in love with a treasure that, made of light, was impervious to the determinism of space and time. And how marvelous, how perfectly apt, that the immortals who loitered, who loosened the knots of their ties, who eternally smoked those *chibi* smokestacks (assuring that those romantic urban nights were always "overcast") were called stars! "Al Pacino," he whispered to himself. "Alpaca Lino, Alpine Piano!" Al Pacino, who in an interview once said: "We weren't actors. We were lamps."

BUT THEN

Just as Mic was recalling the marvelous guy smoking alone in the dark, singing for someone who would never come, Quiver descended from her hamok *with her book,* the book she had only recently mentioned, the book she had—until then—kept jealously close and hidden away. The book that had been left under a bench, a book written by Julio Cortázar, who—as so many (most everybody, actually), had been forgotten. "Listen," said Quiver, and she began to read:

> *This hour that can arrive sometimes outside*
> *all hours, a hole in the net of time,*
> *this way of being between, not above or*
> *behind but between,*
> *this orifice hour to which we gain access in*
> *the lee of other hours, of the immeasurable life*
> *with its hours ahead and on the side, its time for*
> *each thing, its things at the precise time,*
> *to be in a hotel room or on a platform, to be*
> *looking at a shop window, a dog, perhaps*
> *holding you in my arms, siesta love or half*
> *asleep, glimpsing in that patch of light through*
> *the door that opens onto the terrace, in a green*
> *gust the blouse you took off to give me the faint*
> *taste of salt trembling on your breasts . . .*

"Sometimes," Quiver continues, "I imagine us being between; I imagine what Cortázar calls the *sargassum of time* is the shallow sea of space-time and its galaxies that we navigate, quik by quik in our Wobble. And sometimes I recall my time with my lover as once we were *outside all hours,* how our embrace gave us access to ourselves. How we were safe in that embrace. And when I read these words that will always belong to Cortázar and now also belong to me, I imagine that my lover and I met not in a hallway on the Moon, but in a room in a once beloved terrestrial city named Paris, a place I always imagined slick with rain. But no, he tells us the sun is out, it enters the room along with a gust of wind. A warm wind, a green wind. Is it green because the trees beyond the terrace are green? Or is the lover's blouse, silk, I imagine, green, and so light it moves in the wind, a gentle wind, when she lifts it from her body?

"Ah! Mic! How could he have known, and so long ago, too—this man named Julio Cortázar, a man who, before he died, you may recall, is said to have looked like a lion— that the *animal earth* (his words), the vegetal, mineral earth, an earth of rain, of sunlight, of seas tasting of salt, would, after a cascade of catastrophes, *suffocate in a slow stillness,* a relentless stillness, disrupted only by the rock that continues to fall from deep space even now. A cascade of catastrophes variously named: The Burnout, The Washout, The Scouring, The Scaling, The Noise, and, lastly, The Scattering."

TELL ME ALL YOU WISH TO TELL ME

As the cycle opens, Mic, attentive to her in what could be called a "human" way, sees Quiver awaken with a burden of sadness. He approaches her thoughtfully, asks "May I orbit you, Quiv? Just for a moment?"

Knowing this is the very thing he likes to do when feeling "close" to her, she nods. Around and around he goes, until coming to a full stop and taking care not to *crowd her,* he says, "Please, Quiv. Tell me all that you wish to tell me. Tell me everything you wish to share with me at this current quik in time. Tell me about the things I have not witnessed. Tell me something that is not on my Swift Wheel."

"Ah, Mic," Quiver sighs, caressing the top of what stands in for his head, "I woke up remembering something that happened Elsewhere after we had been established long enough for several generations of envelope children to have reached adolescence. At that time the atmosphere was stable—an extraordinary achievement. The air—identical to First World's when it maintained galaxies of creatures interwoven. Now this seems unimaginable!"

"I can imagine it!" Mic spouts. "For I have seen the penguins in their multitudes and always dressed for the Oscars! The gorgeous megalithic cities of the termites—that immeasurable brain! The fox running with her young, the moat rats circumventing the Louvre in Paris in the light of the Moon! These have I seen on my Swift Wheel and more! The whole of Nature, those perishable shapes, the clouds alive with birds—"

"Yes," Quiver sighs. Is silent.

"Please continue, Quiv!" Mic says apologetically. "I just get so excited!"

"The Department of Biotechnology and Deep Memory had been recurring lovely little insects named butterflies—"

"Yes! Yes! I have seen them! On my Swift Wheel! Upgleaming! I have seen them gestating—as you did, Quiv! Awakening from their heavy slumber with sudden wings! Unfolding like blossoms. Vibrating, Quiv, as they tasted the air for the first time! Aroused! Just as all the creatures— the parrot breaking from its shell, the wolf spilling from its womb—awoke aroused! So I have seen them kindled by the sun's sweet fire. They are wet as they break free, and they quiver! Come to think of it, Quiv—this must be why they named you as they did! Quiver! Why are you crying?"

"I, too, have seen them, and often, in the Lights. But the Lights are no longer what they were. Everything has been reimagined—"

"*I know!* All the creatures are *chibi*! But—you were telling a story, Quiv, and I broke in, I forked up unbelievably and I am so sorry! How can you put up with me?"

Quiver barely hears this outburst, recalling all that had happened. "We were informed that a surprise Rekindling was to take place in the public square. Everything had been prepared in secrecy, and we did not know what to expect. There was music, an orchestra playing an updated version of one of Phys Chem's groundbreaking hits."

"Longitudinal List?"

Quiver ignores him, continues: "The butterflies were released in their many thousands, rivers of them, white and gold and green. The children had no idea what they were seeing. Overcome with terror they shouted out and, in their attempts to flee, struck out at one another. Some fell and were trampled. And some seized rocks and hurled them at the sky."

SAILING FASTER

Sailing faster than light (yet in their Bubble they can still *see* the light!) and seemingly motionless, looking up into the eye of the Plonk Sidereal Atlas in silence, they sit back as in all directions bright things in the throes of darkest night, things made of shadow and light, things having succumbed to shadow, having resurged from seas of helium ashes, from forests of kinetic misfortune, having survived mournful wastelands of formaldehyde, perished in inclement estuaries of psychoactive salts, slide past. Something very like an errant brass doorknob rips through their Wobble faceside to backside too quickly to be detected. Briefly they are detained in an ocean of snaggletoothed string that, undulating, causes the fabric of space to billow, to rise to dizzying heights, to fold over them, tuck them in—so that they are snug and unaware of everything that transpires around them. In this way they proceed in safety, withstanding a shower of iron boulders each the size of a moon; make their way unscathed through galaxies that contain nothing but the highly abrasive cinders of stars; are oblivious to an attack of rockets the size of needles and as deadly as the stings of radioactive hornets; escape the embrace of a singularity circumvented by neon canisters; surf an ocean of diamonds served up with crushed ice; awaken on a helium porch studded with the frass of dead meteors to witness an electric storm so monumental its flashes of lightning illuminate an ongoing future moment. Yet, their curiosity was never quenched, even if they were both haunted by their origins, one the issue of an envelope and one *made* (yet, as was Quiver, of matter) on a palpable moon that if now gone, once mattered in the scheme of things.

LUCK

It begins to rain. Everything glistens, looks sticky. She runs the secondary loops. The redhead is nowhere to be seen. This running that gets her nowhere exasperates her.

She asks questions she has never asked. Is the redhead a virtual version of a real woman? An actress? Is she somehow iconic, animating virtual spaces throughout the galaxies, running with countless others? Is she an avatar of a player whose purpose is to disseminate confusion? Are their encounters the spin-off of a program intended to torment her? Or could they be the outcome of chance? Could they be—as she had imagined—*lucky*? Does this word—*lucky*—have a place in the Lights? Are their encounters random? Are they synchronized in ways that remain mysterious?

What does Quiver know of such encounters? Of hazard and luck? Once, wandering the hallways on the Moon, she ran into a cat. She called to it, spoke to it softly. She got down on her knees. The cat ran to her and rubbed against her, its little cries awakening something new within her. It rolled on its back as soon as she began to caress it, rocking from side to side, its feet in the air. Overcome with an exquisite feeling of torpor, she stroked its belly, and when she made to caress its neck, it gently took her finger between its teeth, gazing into her eyes and purring all the while. Now running in the illusion of rain and thinking back on this, she wonders again what it might have been like to live among the creatures. Mic's Swift Wheel hints at a wealth of something essential that continues to elude her. The only first-hand evidence she has of the vanished world—aside from the book, the cat, and a smattering of meaningless things—has been crushed and melted.

There was a cigar-shaped asteroid that they had visited briefly, comprising the highly compressed remains of a mall devoted to horse gear, pets, sex bots, and a *hardware*. Before Burnout, sex bots, Mic explained, had replaced people in brothels and any number of things—marriages, offices, the army, sports teams. If you married one, it came with its own "ambiance," music, and furniture. Many of these quickly became irrelevant, replaced by the Lights.

The cigar-shaped asteroid was a glassy granola studded with birdcages, cat trees, seed balls, sex bots, positioning cuffs, shock absorbers, restraints, bind cages, bondage bars, hot glue sticks, flexisnakes, and waterboards.

But the Swift Wheel. It revealed so much more. It implied something that had no name, yet mattered very much. Something that had everything to do with the tangible density of the incomprehensible. And yet, as precious as it was, the Swift Wheel was also reductive, was impoverished. All it offered was a way of knowing from afar. In its own way it was something like a mass of compressed objects in the shape of a cigar.

To comprehend Mic's gigantic album of everything, to comprehend the Lights, it would take a lover. It would take a lover, Quiver thinks, to wander the city streets, the evening streets, the autumn paths, the summer gardens, the rubble of war—to understand them. And to ask the questions such as: In the streets, were the people safe among themselves? Did the streets ring out with laughter? Just what was it like to sit beneath the sky in a little green boat on a lake? Did the birds fly over the oceans? The mountains? The deserts? The seas? And what of luck? Is this how people found one another? Because they were lucky?

THE BRIGHTER ERG COMPACTION

Feeling somewhat giddy, they penetrate the lesser-known ring of the Brighter Erg Compaction, where once the great Rimsy Grimes had vanished after a series of manic and incomprehensible bleats. The ring sparkled around them, causing a special mood. Mic, buoyant, entertained Quiver with a cascade of vanishing acts—now indistinguishable from Food Face, the overhead lumens, her hamok, the Lesser Thrusting Underbottom Retriever, its blocked girdle, Redding's Afterthought, the forking Corner Cabinet, the Forward Brunt, Underwood's Underhammer and Residue, the Babelocity Decipherment Coil. So taken up are they in this game they neglect Oversight Outlook and are surprised to see a swarm of bots the size of sublunar bees collecting what Quiver recognizes at once as Irradiated Radical Trilibitium that has pearled and adhered to the Plonk Sidereal Atlas Space Eye in quantity. The bots fill their scooter barrels so speedily that the Trilibitium is at once overtaken by the tiny bots in their trillions. The spectacle is mesmerizing. When prodded, Mic leaps into service, scrambling to the Zephyr Equipment Grid, scooping up the coupled disorganizer hose system, and vaporizing the bots with Wingbat's Solvent, which—as the bots tumble into an accelerated backdraft—triggers the Dome

Sucker. In under a quik, the hold is packed with neat bricks of precious Irradiated Radical Trilibitium and a scattering of the equally precious but lesser known Permeable Zinc Blasterite!

To celebrate, Quiver waxes Mic's dexter tinplate—a thing not easy to do, but for which he is grateful. He, in return, and after much thought, and having meticulously explored each and every food vent and reflected upon the egg floss and brines, and in the guise of a beautiful geisha— the notorious Hell—serves Quiver a supper of what he assures her is yellowtail sashimi and a steaming bowl of udon noodles with fish cake. At first she is frightened of the noodles, having never seen them before. But when Mic lifts the chopsticks to her mouth and delicately places a noodle on her tongue, a noodle fragrant and slippery, sopping with a rich reconstructed seaweed broth, she sighs with pleasure. She thinks the redhead is like a delicious udon noodle—a savant coupling of atomic particles and inspired dreaming.

That night she will sleep like a child, will awaken to the sound of a cock crowing (Emu Park neighbors a small private farm), which stirs something very like a memory of a time when the lost world was awakened by its avian tribes—the cocks, the crows, the magpies' inscrutable complaints, the symphonic songbirds speaking righteousness directly to the human heart.

(It was the cock's crow that long ago had startled the infant Julio Cortázar in his crib, who—even before he had the words to say it—intuited an emblematic twinning between the cry of the cock and mortality. Upon hearing the crowing of the cock he recognized with a shudder his inevitable isolation and finitude, that he was his very own strange stranger—and growing stranger by the minute!)

QUIVER'S LONGING (AM LOCUS)

Gracefully folded into her hamok, Quiver says: "Mic. I am overcome with longing. I am longing for a sky that never stops moving. I am longing for cumulus clouds; I am longing for a buttermilk sky.

"I am longing for a clamor of children. Lamplight in a cabin by a river on a fall evening. To pick oranges from a tree. I am longing to see a freshly laid egg. A river of fresh water enter a salty ocean. The animals of Africa. Above all: A tiger! But also bees! Pollinating flowers! A beetle making its way across a bank of moss.

"I am longing for a small planet, a green planet, a blue planet. I could use some city congestion. I could use a cantaloupe, an artichoke, a *microscope*! If we had a microscope, we could, at the very least, watch things moving about!"

"*I* move about!" Mic says it defensively. "I may not 'be alive'—but I am as alive as I *was intended to be;* I do my best, and—"

Admirably, Quiver unfolds, leisurely steps down from her hamok, languidly moves toward Mic, and, seductively, *in human fashion,* gently caressing what stands in for the top of his head, says: "Dearest Micosan. We have been through this a thousand times. You know how much I appreciate your bountiful—*bountiful!* Mic!—capacities. I am stir-crazy is all. I am needing to move about. I am not fed up with your company, but my own."

"Ah," says Mic, filling the sounds of Home Free with Habib Koité. "You need this."

Together, they gaze up at the Plonk Sidereal Atlas. An abundant number of significant destinations litter the path forward. Far dexter a planet appears blinking. "What is it?" Quiver asks just as the Atlas pings, clears its sound box, and speaks:

You are swiftly approaching AM LOCUS, the jewel of a magnificent helical galaxy, the breathing shrapnel, lava, and rock of First Beginnings.

"Oh, forking delirious," sighs Quiver.

AM LOCUS, the Atlas continues, *is the very planet where the first seeds of extraterrestrial multigenesis—conceived and elaborated by Rosalind Von Pfeffertitz—were made manifest!*

"Von Pfeffertitz!" Quiver mumbles. "I have heard of her!"

Who has not heard of Von Pfeffertitz! the Atlas continues. *Her unprecedented collection of genetic variants survived terrestrial collapse. It is here, on AM LOCUS, that the process of multigenesis was not only perfected but also accelerated by Von Pfeffertitz's brain after her demise!*

Quiver winces. "Am I the only one in the universe who finds this drivel aggravating?" she asks Mic. "And *look*— see the date there? This drivel was imbedded ages ago—so who knows what's ahead of us!" She gasps as the Atlas's Space Eye is, in its entirety, overtaken by a virtual brain as wrinkled as the skin of what was once called a Shar-Pei— not that they could know it.

"This," says Quiver decisively, "is not an option." Mic, too, is not eager to get any closer. He, too, is stretched to his limits and out of sorts. His ferroelectric transducer barely glows, and he notices an alarming surge in the oxygen vacancy, a sudden decline in the Wobble's dialectic permittivity.

"All systems are faltering!" Quiver shouts as, despite their best efforts, they are irresistibly drawn to AM LOCUS, its unwanted mysteries and dubious artifact—Von Pfeffertitz's brain.

The Atlas's high-resolution spectroradiometer compounds their frustration, for now they see every knurl, pock, cyst, and gyre of that troubled terrain and the grim towers of a campus built of extemporaneous and biologically modified (and they could not be uglier or more cheesy) printed potluck pavers, tiles, and bricks. So powerful is the planet's magnetic attraction, Quiver's cheeks, lips, and the lids of her eyes swell so badly that for a quik or two she looks *like a fish* (Mic). As for Mic, he is harassed by corporeal statik, his basal zipper perilously hot. All this settles down, however, as they approach the designated landing strip. A shiver, a shudder, a thump—and they come to a stop. Once hydrated, oiled, and suited, they step out into a manageable frost.

AM LOCUS has a fabricated atmosphere, humid and breathable, unexpectedly dense in the organic compounds of living things once there in profusion, but now long gone. Of the landscape, all that remains are deep creases and ridges gyring in all directions, with barely a trace of biological activity. They note what appear to be wormholes, the dens of small mammals, the sorrowful collapse of any number of greenhouses, an artificial lake in need of water, an array of what might well have been the mounds of disorderly—if innovative—termites.

Mic and Quiver now come to a dusty path that takes them to the abandoned campus directly—a pretentious edifice built of the *detestable potluck* (Mic), its grand front gates askew—and enter a lounge illumed by skylights and furnished with faded sofas, the upholstery overrun by the creatures of Von Pfeffertitz's imagining—all *hopelessly ama sugiru* (Mic)—bushy tailed and smiling. The walls surge with sporadically functioning surface Lights all manifesting clusters of enriched transcriptomic motifs: flossy, fleecy, and google-eyed enough to trigger a hyperglycemic crisis.

A large virtual head now appears suspended in their path, sputtering in fits and starts before managing to cohere. It is the head of Von Pfeffertitz: florid, rosy cheeked, and round as a beach ball. *Welcome* it says in any number of languages, known and unknown, imminent, inevitable, likely and unlikely. The welcome is apparently endless, and as they have examined the lights and the furniture, they move on to avoiding bloated descriptions of terrains and creatures that for a brief moment flit and soar, swim and surge, bushy tailed and smiling on AM LOCUS.

"Enjoy your stay!" the head calls after them. "Levitating" says Quiver, "like a forking blimp."

"[§€]^~££§§§¥€|!>] Be sure to explore the greater org of Rosenblatt and WeiWeiSing—named after my two husbands, yes! The very husbands who invented and perfected pseudotemporal myeloids! And be sure not to miss the small chamber, its green door—to the dexter as you are leaving—for everything you are about to see began *there*."

Like a silent and old-timey terrestrial firework display, the head appears to explode and then it is gone. It does not take much poking about before they locate the green door. At their approach it opens.

In the middle of a surprisingly generous space that smells—as does everything on AM LOCUS—of rotting potluck, they see a little table made of illuminated surgical crystal and its crystal balloon. Stashed within the balloon is Von Pfeffertitz's brain. Its bathwater is foggy and the balloon's nicatonium diodes are tarnished.

"There it is," says Mic, "suspended in its spoiled soup, disembarrassed of all significant events."

Quiver responds to this little speech by heaving into a virtual aquarium, further compromising the carpet.

Retracing their steps, they find themselves once more in a world expired.

"I suppose," Quiver says sadly, "collapse was inevitable. After all, everything she and her husbands experimented with was isolated from its realms, its tribes, and from itself. Everything they touched was made singular, was made lonely, without roots or context. Just as I—"

"Are you weeping?" Mic asks, revolving around her like a little planet as is his wont. "Oh! Quiver! Oh! *Dear* Quiv!" As he revolves, Mic gathers speed, warming the two of them. This warming is beneficial, and although they both imagine

Mic's tendency to revolve when Quiver is down is the outcome of a profoundly united and spontaneous gesture, he is, according to the experts, in fact, *wired* to behave this way. In any case, the gesture reestablishes the bond between them. It activates her adrenals and his top rotors.

MARZIPAN TEA

AM LOCUS behind them, and on their way to Gladiolus, they are briefly detained in a nautilus glitch. Coiled into a flat spiral, its segmented crystallized chambers separated by ditches, they are made to wander until colliding with a tearoom occupied by angels who are up to no good. Not only are they lounging on antique rugs like sluts, they are sharing their karaoke machine and marzipan with archons. Mic takes note that the angels flash their naked dorsal palps and the archons are dressed in dubiously harvested ostrich skin jackets. Their horns are stained scarlet; their bitter lips are black with bile.

You are on your way to Gladiolus, the Atlas informs Quiver and Mic directly, just as they are ejected from the glitch by a sudden (and most welcome) mesoblastic detonation. *The planet has an accessible atmosphere with a crisp, dry mouthfeel and a clay body. Gladiolus is known for its one outstanding gladiola—the largest blossoming flower in the universe, which, to the despair of botanists across the galaxy, has toppled over.*

GLADIOLUS

In the beginning, Mic had been wired to the dialects of bees whose symphonies echoed the intimate embrace of space and time. Quiver awakens to the sound of star litter fizzing and popping. She has been dreaming of bees, has often seen them dancing in the Lights. Mic is occupied in his favorite spot beside the perpetually humming ice machine. It is exciting to be surfing the rings of a new planet, now visible, bathed in its sun's early light.

The Wobble lands without incident on a hill of white clay. "Looks like a perfect terrain for the rover," says Mic. Off he goes to fetch Walter Thicke from storage. They set off in an unexpectedly smoky atmosphere beneath clouds the color of welts. Wire birds agitate the air, snatching up flies. These give off a metallic shine, their keys held tightly in their paws. Because the birds are made of wire, Quiver comments she can see the flies' attempts to escape.

"There is no sound as dismal as the sound of a trapped fly," says Quiver. "It is the sound of hopelessness," says Walter Thicke. "It is the sound particles and quarks make trapped inside an atom. How eager they are to get out!"

"How can you possibly know this?" Quiver, in a bad mood, complains.

"Because it is how I feel," he answers. "How I feel parked in storage."

Unsettled by this revelation, Mic attempts to mollify Walter by asking him what he thinks the birds and the flies are made of. Walter's Rolodex has a good handle on minerals and the languages of the Outer Galaxies.

"The flies' little feet, the birds' beaks—these are made of Fistula Green. The planet is—as so many in this galaxy—rich in Cataclysmite and Fistula Green. The surface is of white clay; it is all clay," continues Walter, "but for the—"

"Cataclysmite," says Quiver impatiently, "and Fistula Green."

"You have stolen my words," says Walter, sadly. Just then they see the locals parading toward them, their faces, feet, and hands made of fired clay. "The clay is local," Walter Thicke hastens to tell them, "and their felt bodies are stuffed with toxic seeds. The one with the big belly supported by a truss of some sort is Top Rancor—a senior official. We have no alternative but to submit to his demands."

"But they are *dolls*!" Quiver erupts. "Their features are painted on! Their forking eyes are lifeless!"

"Yet they are fixedly looking," says Walter. "Yet they can see."

"And their *brains*?" asks Quiver. "What are their brains made of?"

"Snow," he tells her. "Their brains are made of snow." He now proves himself invaluable as, without introductions or snacks, they are bludgeoned by Top Rancor's endless discourse; it boils down to this: *They must obtain their permits at once.*

Mic and Quiver are given a pail and a shovel. Obtaining permits entails being led on leashes across a mournful landscape to a specific bank of clay at the bottom of a steep ravine, at the far side of an outcropping of slick hills. Having supplied themselves with clay, they are made to go at once to a workstation at an indeterminate distance, manufacture their permits in molds supplied for this purpose, fire them in a kiln fueled by dry thistles that they must collect themselves and artfully bind together.

Once the kiln has cooled, they unmold their permits, carry them to a certain obelisk, and, standing in its shadow, attend yet another discourse on the need to carry their permits—each the shape and size of a good-sized brick—with them at all times. Any false move on their parts, any nicks in their bricks . . . *will be punished by having their permits hurled at them from a tidy distance.*

Next they find themselves forced to submit to an imbecilic litany of petty denunciations:

> *You have arrived at Gladiolus, a sovereign*
> *state, without permission, nor have you*
> *requested a permit, despite the fact that upon*
> *Top Rancor's obelisk, it is inscribed without*
> *ambiguity that those who set foot on the white*
> *clay of Gladiolus must carry a permit exactly*
> *as one carries one's face at all times. All visitors,*
> *prior to their arrival, are required to study the*
> *laws and be prepared to arrive wearing rush*
> *brushes on the rims of their hats so as to be*
> *recognized as aliens. Should these precautions*
> *be ignored, the visit will be brief and tedious to*
> *the extreme.*

Having said this, Top Rancor loses interest in them and takes off in the direction of the obelisk. (Walter Thicke informs them that Top Rancor leases a penthouse apartment at the very top.) They are now prodded and poked down a path in a new direction. Walter Thicke, who has stood by all the while, is made to stay behind.

"I want to ride in Walter Thicke!" Quiver shouts. "You cannot—"

Even though the dolls cannot open their mouths, nor do they appear to have teeth, she is silenced by being bitten on the cheek.

It is not long before they see the first cage. Sturdy enough, on the verge of unapproachable, it is woven of an abrasive grass. Coming close, they are made to look inside. They see a doll holding a grass cage on its lap, a smaller doll within holding its own caged doll, who holds a cage. They are given a magnifying glass and, inevitably, the caged doll's doll holds a caged doll on its lap, its own doll caged, and so on. Turn by turn, every one of the dolls stares at them fixedly, with widely spaced and uncannily sighted eyes.

"I hear their heads," whispers Quiver, "swarming with flies." For this she is ferociously poked. The dolls are so fearsome they can do nothing but follow them up one mournful hill after another to examine cages containing more dolls, to gaze into the cages with their magnifying glasses, to feel the flies swarming within their minds ever more loudly—as meanwhile the sky above them changes color, turns a rotten tangerine, an abraded yellow, and Fistula Green—the colors of a bad bruise. They progress farther with no refuge in sight, nor consolation, rudely poked and prodded all the while, more cages coming into view, and after that yet more.

As they reach the summit of yet another hill, the sky yawns with such amplitude it swallows itself. There is nothing but darkness all around them. They stand in this darkness until stunned by a terrific knock to the head; they are abandoned, sprawling on the white clay, as the stars of that dreadful place watch them from the yawning that has released them, pressing so forcefully down that had Quiver and Mic been aware, they would not have been able to stand or, for that matter, roll over or whisper.

I cannot say how long the night lasted, but when it was over they awakened packed into Walter Thicke, whose motor was quietly purring. They returned to the Wobble at once where Walter was decommissioned and tucked into cargo. *Dolls in cages,* Quiver ponders, her mood so dark she can barely think. *Dolls in cages all the way down.* Something incomprehensible, yet also familiar. A memory from which she is fleeing. *It was like that on the Moon,* she recalls with a shudder. *When the children were all vanishing within themselves.*

REMEMBER

"Remember," Quiver asks Mic, sometime later and deep in the middle of nowhere, "when everyone was listening to *Brains on Plastic*?"

"I loved *Brains on Plastic*!" Mic cries enthusiastically. "So twisted!"

"I hated *Brains on Plastic*. So sick, Mic! But I was crazy for *Brains on Bees*." Upon reflection she adds: "We must take better care of Walter." And then, walking to the middle of Home Free, Quiver surprises Mic by singing the *Brains on Bees* classic:

> ### Helium
> *Breathing helium*
> *alive as anything*
> *in the real air.*
> *There we are*
> *in the nowhere*
> *when*
> *something familiar*
> *throws us to the floor*
> *again*
> *our gums bleeding*
> *for lack of something*
> *or other*
> *that's not here.*
> *Not ever.*

LINGER LONGER

"What's that pretty galaxy just a stone's throw away?" Quiver asks as they sail past what appears to be a fog of crushed bone.

"Elictpic," says Mic, quick as ever. "We are fast approaching its hottest star, Meander. Meander is made of meat, Blasterite, black marbles, and Bitumen. Its two planets are Linger Longer and Glass Ceiling."

"Linger Longer sounds nice," Quiv murmurs dreamily. "It sounds like a place with a spa."

"Linger Longer," Mic informs her, his Swift Wheel flashing orange, "uses its beard—"

"Forking unbelievable! I see its beard!"

"—to snag everything in its reach and stuff it—"

"Forget it. What about Glass Ceiling?"

"Shaped like a snow globe . . ."

"A snow globe?"

"A glass ball with a flat bottom, and in the middle—not sure what that is in the middle."

"We shall stay clear of Linger Longer's beard! Wow!" says Quiver. Mic performs a sudden and magnificent wing over, a masterful fork over, a peerless fair shake, coin toss, and grand slam.

"Why?" Quiver moans, her face in her hands. "Why is our universe so scary?"

"Walter Thicke blames the angels," says Mic. "Told me they are nothing but fops. They live on marzipan and have the minds of moths."

"I suggested he join us in Home Free," says Quiver, "but he prefers to spend his time in cargo with my abandoned Zanx Fixer—a very recent encounter although they have shared cargo for an age. 'We both go bonkers over the same stuff!' he told me, visibly excited—and boy, did he get into it! Linguistics! 'Isn't it interesting, Quiver,' he said, 'that on Agiato, they toss their carefully preserved baby teeth into the air, letting them fall where they may; that the reading of the teeth is said to be like reading the liver. On Agnoetae, they act similarly with the empty shells of snails, and on Annona, they boil wooden alphabet blocks in wine and set them on the floor. On Aristippus, they speak only during courtship—if in a manner familiar to us—but once they are wedded they clam up—although some are said to be fluent biters. On Barbaros, they communicate by means of art-fully gassed atmospheres and intercalating molecules. The wee folks on Bandergap toss nano-electrical lattices at one another. And! Guess what, Quiver,' he said to me (and never have I seen Walter Thicke so excited!), 'some languages are glottological and some are powerful defoliants!'"

SOMETHING UNIQUE AND UNSCRUTABLE

Time in the Wobble goes nowhere. Quiver loses track of it. Often it seems that all that had transpired on the Moon long before she and Mic had become a team based on Elsewhere, has only just happened—it is all so vivid in her mind. Whenever she tells Mic about the Moon, these memories are further heightened. This cycle she tells him about a crop of pocket infants all unable to sustain a kiss. For them a loving glance caused the greatest anguish. All their lives they remained cloistered, the walls, ceilings, and floors of their rooms faced with wadding. They grew slowly toward puberty—a destination about which they knew nothing and would never know anything—entertaining themselves with soft and softly murmuring robots in pallid colors. These were shaped like cubes, pyramids, spheres, and stars. Not long after adolescence, the children's marrow became infected with something unique and unscrutable.

It was during this time that Quiver left for Elsewhere. By then Base was the size of what had once been the Bronx. Not long after, Noise obliterated Earth and her moon—its impact such that even Elsewhere had been buffeted as a sound they had never heard before crowded their ears—a sound Mic recalls that brought to mind a monumental glass bell filled to the brim with tacks and struck with a tuning fork. A submerged lake surfaced in response—Mic, too, remembers this. Elsewhere, shortly thereafter, was ringed by a seething gumbo of everything—the very rings Mic and Quiv would mine for their serviceable amalgams of Indiana limestone and the rest—including the occasional brass doorknob and a waffle iron.

As Quiver recalls these things, Mic, double tasking, attends to her every word, sometimes interjecting: "I had no idea!" or "I remember that too, Quiv!" He is steeped in an investigation into sound, including big noises, and their place in the universe. "Just listen to this!" he exclaims the instant Quiver grows quiet, "These are the words of the mystic Sin the Androgyne:"

> *Just as the Initial Manifestation of a universe*
> *begins with a terrible roar, so are Endings*
> *heralded by an ear-piercing din. If Silence is*
> *Virtue, then, the cosmos, its rocks and races, its*
> *tribes, mansions and slums, its caged tigers and*
> *toddlers, its bathtubs brimming with the bones*
> *of innocents soaking in lime—is depraved.*

"What if there is no intrinsic meaning to the universe?" Quiver whispers it.

"Well," Mic replies, "that would explain everything."

A LUSTER

Once again and for the last time, Quiver returns to the Lights. A floating brain, a cohort of toxic dolls, a stalking tattoo, archons and angels at tea—the senselessness of her destiny in an incomprehensible universe has her wondering, What is it all *about*? What am I *about*? I suppose I am about my longing, she decides as she runs the familiar path. My longing for a lover and for a home. And Mic shares in this longing. This longing is our shared aboutness!

She thinks that living in the Wobble is living in a robot's world, not a human's world. No wonder she feels so *out of it,* so unfit, so alone. So forking grumpy all the time. Her world had been taken from her long before she was released, squawling, from her pitiful envelope hanging from its wire only to be hooked up to a robot in a fur jacket with a rubber nipple. "I need a planet I can walk on," she says out loud. "I need to wake up in a morning to a sun's light, and sleep in the dark of night, beneath a familiar moon and stars I can recognize and call by name."

Running eases her heartache, the thrumming in her mind, her chronic perplexity and surging impatience. And then something flashes between the leaves for one bright instant in time. She recognizes a luster tattoo of a kind ubiquitous on Elsewhere during her last furlough, when she and Mic had delivered a stunning collection of crystalized

Melanogasters—the very crystalized Melanogasters essential to the successful acceleration of cytovect fiber torsion pendulum turntables—one of their more successful assignments.

Quiver takes off away from the path and into the trees. It is *she*—the fabulous elusive creature, the redhead, a luster riding the jade of her left shoulder, flashing as if in extremity, as if signaling a disaster, but there *is no disaster*—only a significant message indicating that she is not alone in the seeing, but that she, too, is seen. As Quiver runs, her own luster—a dragonfly—responds with a soft gleaming in concert with the other luster, a crazy cat luster that changes color until their colors coincide—the redhead's gold crazy cat and her own dragonfly, now both gleaming, warm to the touch and pulsing. Quiver is submerged in a sweet incandescence as her wrist is gently seized by another hand.

And now they meet; they stand face to face. The redhead's eyebrows are trimmed in the manner called *mothwing*—once popular on Elsewhere when the band Soma Cosmic and its lead singer, Semiconducting Metallic, had influenced intergalactic fashion. Her eyes are green, no, they are violet; they are a violet green speckled with chalcedony. Her heart leaping in her ears, Quiver dives into those crazy eyes as the redhead takes her chin gently between her hands—how soft they are!—and kisses her, causing their lusters to flare up and incandesce. Before vanishing the redhead whispers:

"See you on Trafik!"

THE ENDOCYCLIC QUASAR MASS

Eager to proceed, Quiver awakens with expectation. But before they reach Trafik, they must surf the Endocyclic Quasar Mass, a tumultuous region unsettled by a throng of transgressive stars that—despite a flashing and most attractive appearance—are, according to the angels, "of corruptible nature, crooked, anarchic, and treacherous."

"But that's nonsense," says Mic. "You and I know that the stars are without will or self-awareness; without agenda or purpose. Space, just as the oceans, has its rogue waves, riptides, tsunamis, and whirlpools. I am about to roll us a barrel and make us a hole to slide through. Hold on, Quiv!"

Already she can feel the foam faceside coalesce and compress, how backside the thruster labors against an unfathomable absence, feel it vibrate so violently it threatens to chew its own teeth as then in under a quik, they are scaled down to the ultramicroscopic, eyeballed by the busy slit of a split atom. It is tough! thinks Quiver. All this travel, all this expanding and contracting! All these peculiar places and questionable encounters!

They rebound unscathed in a flood of buttery light that Mic suggests is an early manifestation of the ecstasy they are certain to experience shortly. Home Free is drenched in a divine music as they surge forth in a spume of sparks that, yielding, delivers them to the longed-for threshold. Trafik is now within reach!

ARRIVAL

And there it was! Moments away, a red and green planet rich in Verdurian and Libidion, Ardente. And there were other minerals on Trafik as well, such as Inorganite, Inanimite, and, above all, Conundrum—of which there was a seemingly unlimited supply.

Mic activated the Wipers that, in their multitudes, set about to scour the Wobble's outer integument as they sped past Citronový Sorbet—Trafik's midget sun (and Trafik was a midget planet) recognized as such by what was once the Czech Republic just prior to the First Scouring (quoth Mic). They landed in Guest Parking without a hitch; leaving Walter Thicke in storage they set off on foot. Quiver wore a dashing Musk Breathalaton in a nostril, a snug set of surface overalls zippered in platinum, her *endless legs* (Mic) shod in vintage moon boots. Inspired by the painter Arcimboldo, Mic stepped out cuirassed in Al Pacino's plumbing—an innovative synthesis of pipes and sinks that propelled him into the future of fashion, a quantum leap that was received by the youthful and transcosmical crowds of intergalactic students of cosmology, the Extreme Sciences, Molecular Revisioning, Vital and Arbitrary Disruption, Trans Worlds Without Impediment, and so on—who were all on summer break. Trailblazing, Mic, in his element, dominated streets free of bureaucrats, missionaries, dogmatists, and syndicate crime lords in exile who, having found each other, had settled down for eternity poolside and in game rooms where they wiled away the hours playing Table Lights' versions of Deep Fry, Snatch Luck, and Poor Bastard. Meanwhile, in the streets, cloned cows pissed milk into fountains of Libidion rimmed with mugs. The beautiful mug washers wore boots heeled in Ardorite, so that as they ran up and down the cobbled streets to retrieve a mug or to offer a kiss, they made an irresistible music unique to that place, rich in roulades, incidental notes, diatomic intervals, and an artful use of rubato. This music is called "Catch and Snatch," and later in the day, "Damn!"

The streets were lined with everbearing bushes of sandwiches, notably ham and swiss, shrimp tacos, and egg salad. Overhead the clouds responded to the laughter in the streets with coursing displays of corrals of sheep, coral reefs, and canyons of cream. Everywhere flocks of birds rose into the air, buttery crusts of sandwiches in their beaks. Mic and Quiver were swept up and away by an afternoon that never ended, had not ever ended, nor would it end, unspooling for entire epochs as far back as could be remembered. Trafik's obscure liturgical literature had long ago given up attempting to answer the questions concerning the planet's origins, such as:

Which came first? The milkmaids or the cows? The mugs or the fountains? When had it been decided that anyone and everyone could drink the milk and eat the sandwiches for free? Was the scattering of the crusts on the pavement a sacred act or a secular one? It was said that the constant back and forth of beings in the streets, the mugs filled and emptied of milk over and over, the rising and fall-ing of the birds, Citronový Sorbet's own spinning—all this was the incontrovertible evidence that the universe was either intentionally or unintentionally *restless.*

And this inherent restlessness! Was it due to random-ness, or an innate longing for answers, for belonging? And was the erotic impulse at the heart of the matter sparking a fundamental, an unstoppable yearning to bring things together, ideas and particles and bodies? And lastly, was Eros a cosmical dragon breathing fire and making it all happen?

MINDFUL DISTRACTIONS

In other words, Mic was in his element. Riding the shoulders of a strapping and trending astroanthropologist, surrounded by the jubilant young scholars, their quantum pectoral bootstraps beaming lectures, panels, and seminars (all were consummate multitaskers)—even as they, in dizzying erotic and existential variety celebrated awareness and yes! *restlessness* (and also restless awareness and aware restlessness), embracing one another's unique manifestations of the boundless forms of desire, each one well aware of the benefits of philosophical detachment when swept up and away in the unfettered embrace of multivarious ecstatic encounters and other kindred phenomena, their minds and bodies (and some had no "bodies" and others wore their "minds" in their lower spines, feet, or ears) unbound or, at least, making an attempt at this unbinding—having ascertained that just because the once beautiful living earth— a powerful exemplar throughout the universe—had been made not only the Mirror of Hell but also its embodiment— that each of them was to perceive everyone else with eyes (peepers, sight holes, ocular navels, antennae, and so on) WIDE OPEN and with the understanding that each of them was the potential vessel of BEING and UNDERSTANDING. And yet! WHAT KEEPS CLOSING IN!? This question, shouted periodically by the crowd, punctuated the pilgrimage to

Pleroma Park, which was the astral hub of MINDFUL DIS-TRACTION. All of them had come from far away, had tackled the passage, the savage estuaries riddled with shattered rock and imploding suns, because they had heard that there was a planet in the universe suspended as it were between air and ether, where every form of the material and virtual and imagined could come together with a fearless and affectionate intention. And now, *here they were!* In Trafik! No doubt about that!

Swallowed up by Trafik's shimmering abundance, Mic, now unrecognizable in a velours burnous, his gametophores erect and softly singing, found himself standing before Al Pacino—as if Al had been waiting for him all that time, eagerly waiting in that ambient intemperance, head to foot in the living velours, waiting to whisper in Mic's very own hearing hole: *What's up?* And this within the green light, the silver shadows, the two of them invisible, an instant away from an embrace, the emerald pneumonic froth of admissibility, peerless and benevolent, enfolding them in an ocean of tenderness punctuated by the sound of love-making as lovers from across the galaxies embraced in their myriad conformations, conformations subverted and upended by ubiquitous moss topcoats, cunning velours bomber jackets, and so on, so that the bearded mollusks of Wazat, having just arrived from the distant galaxy whose name was impossible to know (their language spoken in a frequency so low it generated infinitesimal hypergravity pinholes so powerful they swallowed up the syllables by capillary attraction the moment they were uttered) without hesitation simultaneously solemnized the spindled tortoises and shelled philosophical walruses of Wizz—a planet known for its intemperate heterotrophic lobsters. And there were pilgrims no bigger than bioplasts (come to think of it, maybe they *were* bioplasts!), some initially too large to think of venturing into Trafik's spumous verdure without causing havoc and so had particulated into microbodies, each one at once cumuliformed, castellated, and fleeced.

As you have seen, the wonderful thing about Trafik was that it did not seem to matter where you came from, what epoch you belonged to, if you were a shapeshifter, an anarchic trilobite, or a Melusianne Lioness. Al Pacino, after all, was a figment from a world long vanished. Yet as soon as Mic entered Trafik's green clusterfork, Al Pacino was there, sporting a marvelous Italian suit the color of grass, asking, *What's up?* And that was all it took for Mic to dissolve in irresistible centrifugal delight. *Pass the salt,* Al said caressingly, *I got a fever.* The implications were stunning. When replete, who knows how much later, his software revivified, Mic and Al Pacino embraced one last time with the promise of future encounters, having shared their secrets, their deepest feelings, and their pathway instructions. Mic, overwhelmed with something that approximated emotion so convincingly that had you been there, you would have sworn it was *human,* broke down, his router wipes scrambling into action, his overkey furiously oscillating, his rumpus wafting, so that Al Pacino, touched to the quick, leapt from the bush that had cloaked them in blessed pudicity suggesting Mic remain with him on Trafik thereafter. *Our neurons,* he whispered, *could not have better fired.* And it was true. *I have a cabin in the woods in the mountains,* Al told him. Mic texted Quiver at once. *I am staying on Trafik,* he told her. *If it is interesting, it justifies being there.* (It is funny how, in no time at all, Mic started talking like Al Pacino. He'd say things like: *I used to have a refrigerator. Every time I opened it a bottle of lubricator fell on my foot. I knew I had to buy a bigger refrigerator. Instead I became an astronaut.*)

Mic's text continued:

Quiver, I gotta tell you! We were word hole to word hole, joined in tender congress, as close together as neurons in the mind of a fruit fly or the scales on the wings of a moth (things that Al has described to me that I have diligently found neatly nestled and labeled in my Swift Wheel). This afternoon I discovered that the cycles on Trafik are not mea-sured. Each instant dissolves as it surfaces, unencumbered by time, by all that burdens us when we are running from something or someone and going somewhere (and it doesn't matter where), which means that the moment is bleached by expectation, it loses salt and flavor. Wheras! If madly in love one stays still within the depths of the moment (which is pos-sible, Quiv! I know this now!), the cycles of time fall away, are but a mist; one dwells within an atmosphere! I am speaking of an Aroused Tranquility! Yes! That's it exactly!

But this knowledge, Quiver, comes with a price! I mean, I paid for it terribly. In the instants before my encounter with Al, submerged in Trafik's immense green-lit immoder-acy, I mislaid myself in a way I can only call human—*and for one brief instant (and what are we if not the cogni-zant vehicles of the instant?), I recognized the limits of my* capacity to feel (or so I thought)—but what is far worse, I heard a voice cricketing from somewhere deep within my nerve net that said I was a gizmo—yes, that rusty trope! That ancient terror! And what's more, it was the voice of another gizmo, a gizmo I did not know, had not been introduced to; a gizmo that considered I was verging on the obsolete, so outdated I was barely able to withstand the assault of ongoing updates! This intruder was periodically violating my boundaries without my knowledge! Imagine, Quiv, if you awakened from a nap only to discover someone had tampered with your neurons while you were sleeping! But then! Guess what! When Al Pacino stood there beside me and said: I know you from somewhere, I swear I felt something, my nerve net got bolted, my endoplasmic barometer ignited, my mood lifted, and I felt joy! Yes! I now know what it is to feel joy!

At the very end of his text, Mic added a list:

> I have visited a planet where they suicide by
>   gagging on hard-boiled eggs.
> A planet souped from pole to pole with
>   flatulence.
> A planet in convulsions caused by unbridled fits
>   of temper.
> A planet whose most evolved species grow
>   asparagus on their heads.
> An asteroid the size and conformation of a lima
>   bean that turned out to be a lima bean.
> A planet named Desquamata; a phlegmatic
>   planet.

An asteroid belt inhabited by scholars counting
the hairs of a lesser God's beard.

A planet named Benzofuroxan that provides
travelers with generous helpings of spaghetti
and meatballs.

An asteroid in the grips of a tyrant named
Buster Quimsy who liked to be beaten with
logs of frozen honey.

A planet of cognizant marbles that do nothing
but slam into one another.

A planet made of cake inhabited by fairy
godmothers in their bathrobes.

An asteroid belt flaming with salamanders.

A fast food concession in orbit named Pass
On By.

I have seen all this and more. But I have never
seen anything like Trafik!

COZY STREETS

When Quiver received Mic's heartfelt text, she was far from the excitement, wandering Trafik's cozy residential streets, admiring the graceful front porches of a type common in the known universe, the facades of tidy homes built of what she supposed was olivine brick, the roofs artfully thatched with the same modifiable and acoustical moss that so lovingly sheltered the amorous couples in the park. She admired the moss lawns, the whimsical backyard topiaries, the redundant birdbaths and robokitty doors. Such homes enchanted Quiver, who had spent her early years in icy corridors and printed everplast yurts the color of oxidized mustard, and for what seemed an eternity inside the Wobble with Mic sharing one room: Home Free. As she wandered, Quiver recalled a time she and Mic had returned to the Wobble after a lengthy layover on a planet known for its seismic activity. During a tremor, a bottle of Kleinenburg's Buffered Flexwizer had fallen to the floor causing every surface to strobe with luminescence. Off-gassing, the Buffered Flexwizer had compromised Food Face, its dehydrated aspics and freezies. She recalled how Mic had rallied, how his Tackle Kit had sponged forth from its socket, how Home Free had rocked with the happy sound of sponges swarming, scrubbing, and irradiating. Rolling on his rudders, Mic did the laundry, visited the stock room again and again, replenishing Food Face with spontaneous crackers, synchronous raisin clonotypes, extended banana protein saturate, and inflatable figs. *He's a good egg, that Mic,* she thought.

A LIBRARY

Just as Trafik's third moon, Erratum, rises in the afternoon
sky, Quiver takes a turn and, as in a dream, comes upon a
novel stone building of great charm with a large front door,
arches, and columns—arches and columns, things of which
she has no knowledge, nor has she the words. This is the
neighborhood library. During cautiously whispered con-
versations, her lover had told her about First Planet's many
libraries, but of course Quiver had never seen one, nor could
she really fathom its purpose. Curious, she takes a trim garden path to the strange yet inviting, new yet familiar front
door and steps into a large, nearly empty room shimmering with light. It is empty but for the impressive glass snake
at the entrance, holding a glass apple in its mouth, and, at
the center of the room, a glass cabinet filled with glass bees.
Stimulated by the sudden breeze Quiver has released into
the room, these begin to hum homophonically and, beating their glass wings and dancing, to rise up into the air.
A small piece of heavy paper pressed to the glass cabinet
explains that the dances of the bees were once books of a
kind that could be "read." And there is a clay tablet the size
of a small square piece of cake. Its own text reads:

> *Seven days and seven nights did Enkidu,*
> *the wild man, cling to Shammat the whore.*

Quiver thinks she recognizes it, that it is a thing she and Mic had found working the Moon's dizzy rings of compacted materials so very long ago.

Next to the cabinet, an antique Sly Sparks Laser Printer sits on a pedestal, and on a shiny shelf, a number of paper books made by the schoolchildren stand side by side in their colorful covers.

Quiver now sees the librarian sitting at her desk at the far side of the room, so far away it seems she is on the far side of a moon, nearly erased by the constant play of light streaming in from all directions, bounding from wall to wall and ceiling to floor. In this sea of light, the librarian stands, and smiling, her delicate horn nibs gilded and gleaming, walks across the room to greet Quiver with a French kiss—a custom on Trafik as common as pie. Her name is Data Fig. Quiver, unsure if she is actually awake, says to herself: *Behold the librarian!* She says to herself: *I am here! And I am not going anywhere!*

"The most interesting thing we have," Data Fig begins, "is the crystal snake, made by a local craftsman. Its birefringent interacting facets can be read at certain times during the afternoon. It tells the story of The Washout, The Burnout, The Scaling, The Scouring, The Scattering, and The Noise— with brevity and poetic prose. You are surprised to see no books," says Data Fig, "but—apart from the children's book (a project just begun—there are more of these on the way)— thus far it seems Earth was the only place in the galaxies where books flourished. Perhaps one day—"

"I have a book!" Quiver whispers it.

"A book!" Data Fig's eyes fill with tears.

"Long ago," Quiver tells her, "I found it hidden under a bench on the Moon. It was my lover who left it there for me, before she was made to vanish . . ."

Quiver, too, is weeping, as Data Fig reaches for her and holds her close, the library surging with light in a room that is a vessel of light, the two holding one another, their bodies holding the light, as the glass snake's story of deepest shadow is written in light on the library's luminous walls.

"I have a bot named Mic with me," Quiver whispers, still held close in the librarian's embrace. "A bot with a fully functional Swift Wheel, packed full of all kinds of things. But I don't know if his Swift Wheel contains books."

"A Swift Wheel!" Thrilled, Data Fig steps back. "The Swift Wheel always held a vast library! Have you never checked it out?"

"No one ever spoke of it!" Quiver tells her. "I never even thought of it! There was always so much that was entertaining. And I had the Lights. Perhaps because I had been made to fear books, the consequences of owning one, I learned not to think of them. It took me a very long time to open the one I have."

"What is the title?"

"From the Observatory."

"A wonderful title! And the author?"

"Julio Cortázar."

"You will tell your friend Mic to come and see me tomorrow afternoon," says Data Fig. "If he can be made to hook up with my Sly Sparks Laser Printer, a full library is not far away." And she makes a somersault right there on the library floor.

CHRISTOPHER WALKEN ON BEES

Later in the afternoon, Quiver enters the park alone, wanders that green maze of sighs, of adaptable acoustical moss. She fears the redhead is trapped in the Lights—her own inescapable virtuality and that she will never find her. And she explores Trafik's old and new quarters effortlessly, feeling her senses quicken. She choses a pub, its ceiling lamps spinning like moons. Finds a table, a mini *Lights on a Loop* clamped to its top that, the moment she sits down, begins to play:

> ### Christopher Walken on Bees
> *So. Bees. They're funny characters. They move*
>   *around.*
> *Making that noise they make. I have a hunch.*
>   *They're talking*
> *somehow. So. It's not a noise they're making.*
>   *It's just bees. Talking.*

The pub's atmosphere is soaking with music. Drifting down, it fills the air with a gentle fog of sound. Quiver orders a citrus Gender Cracking cocktail and looks around. At the far end of the room there is a small commotion. A crowd of star hoppers, all celebrating the Bad Boys of Blasty's decisive victory in aggravated desk tennis, have stormed the room. A pause, a moment's quiet, and there she is, the redhead, spectacular, translucent, her skin the color of green jade, wearing a tight white suit of derived homeostatic photons, and walking her way, a robokitty neatly tucked beneath her right arm. Never before has Quiver felt so absolutely, irreversibly, made of flesh. This is what it is, she thinks, flushed and rising, to be what Mic calls CHARISMATIZED. The music swells a current pop hit by the Chromatids—*Jelly:*

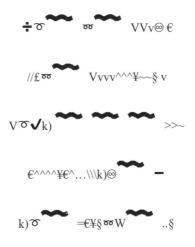

Even before she has a moment to consider it, Quiv and the redhead effortlessly collide, dissolve, and in sweetness adhere—an amalgam of Matter and Light. Another instant and they are entwined, nymphs converging in a sudden turquoise cocoon woven of stardust, mica, and moss—one couple among a multitude suspended from the ceiling. In such ways is love attained on Trafik—that place not above or behind but between; a place where love gains access in the lee of immeasurable life.

After love, the redhead tells Quiver her name is Tremor and her robokitty is Flutter. Quiver expresses her delight in Flutter's fleece and Tremor's everything, including her green skin.

"Everyone who hangs out on Trafik long enough becomes green," Tremor explains. "Soon my little robokitty will be green, too, as, my beloved, will you!" Then, reaching for the sky and yawning, Tremor says, "Hey Quiv! Let's take a run together in the unfolding afternoon's virtuals and realities!"

Coffee House Press began as a small letterpress operation in 1972 and has grown into an internationally renowned non-profit publisher of literary fiction, essay, poetry, and other work that doesn't fit neatly into genre categories.

Coffee House is both a publisher and an arts organization. Through our *Books in Action* program and publications, we've become interdisciplinary collaborators and incubators for new work and audience experiences. Our vision for the future is one where a publisher is a catalyst and connector.

LITERATURE
is not the same thing as
PUBLISHING

Funder Acknowledgments

Coffee House Press is an internationally renowned independent book publisher and arts nonprofit based in Minneapolis, MN; through its literary publications and *Books in Action* program, Coffee House acts as a catalyst and connector—between authors and readers, ideas and resources, creativity and community, inspiration and action.

Coffee House Press books are made possible through the generous support of grants and donations from corporations, state and federal grant programs, family foundations, and the many individuals who believe in the transformational power of literature. This activity is made possible by the voters of Minnesota through a Minnesota State Arts Board Operating Support grant, thanks to the legislative appropriation from the Arts and Cultural Heritage Fund. Coffee House also receives major operating support from the Amazon Literary Partnership, Jerome Foundation, McKnight Foundation, Target Foundation, and the National Endowment for the Arts (NEA). To find out more about how NEA grants impact individuals and communities, visit www.arts.gov.

Coffee House Press receives additional support from the Elmer L. & Eleanor J. Andersen Foundation; the David & Mary Anderson Family Foundation; Bookmobile; Dorsey & Whitney LLP; Foundation Technologies; Fredrikson & Byron, P.A.; the Fringe Foundation; Kenneth Koch Literary Estate; the Matching Grant Program Fund of the Minneapolis Foundation; Mr. Pancks' Fund in memory of Graham Kimpton; the Schwab Charitable Fund; Schwegman, Lundberg & Woessner, P.A.; the Silicon Valley Community Foundation; and the U.S. Bank Foundation.

 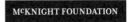

The Publisher's Circle of Coffee House Press

Publisher's Circle members make significant contributions to Coffee House Press's annual giving campaign. Understanding that a strong financial base is necessary for the press to meet the challenges and opportunities that arise each year, this group plays a crucial part in the success of Coffee House's mission.

Recent Publisher's Circle members include many anonymous donors, Patricia A. Beithon, the E. Thomas Binger & Rebecca Rand Fund of the Minneapolis Foundation, Andrew Brantingham, Dave & Kelli Cloutier, Louise Copeland, Jane Dalrymple-Hollo & Stephen Parlato, Mary Ebert & Paul Stembler, Kaywin Feldman & Jim Lutz, Chris Fischbach & Katie Dublinski, Sally French, Jocelyn Hale & Glenn Miller, the Rehael Fund-Roger Hale/Nor Hall of the Minneapolis Foundation, Randy Hartten & Ron Lotz, Dylan Hicks & Nina Hale, William Hardacker, Randall Heath, Jeffrey Hom, Carl & Heidi Horsch, the Amy L. Hubbard & Geoffrey J. Kehoe Fund, Kenneth & Susan Kahn, Stephen & Isabel Keating, Julia Klein, the Kenneth Koch Literary Estate, Cinda Kornblum, Jennifer Kwon Dobbs & Stefan Liess, the Lambert Family Foundation, the Lenfestey Family Foundation, Joy Linsday Crow, Sarah Lutman & Rob Rudolph, the Carol & Aaron Mack Charitable Fund of the Minneapolis Foundation, George & Olga Mack, Joshua Mack & Ron Warren, Gillian McCain, Malcolm S. McDermid & Katie Windle, Mary & Malcolm McDermid, Sjur Midness & Briar Andresen, Daniel N. Smith III & Maureen Millea Smith, Peter Nelson & Jennifer Swenson, Enrique & Jennifer Olivarez, Alan Polsky, Robin Preble, Alexis Scott, Ruth Stricker Dayton, Jeffrey Sugerman & Sarah Schultz, Nan G. Swid, Kenneth Thorp in memory of Allan Kornblum & Rochelle Ratner, Patricia Tilton, Stu Wilson & Melissa Barker, Warren D. Woessner & Iris C. Freeman, and Margaret Wurtele.

For more information about the Publisher's Circle and other ways to support Coffee House Press books, authors, and activities, please visit www.coffeehousepress.org/pages/donate or contact us at info@coffeehousepress.org.

We gratefully acknowledge the following supporters of our 2020 Give to the Max Day campaign:

Nancy Baumoel, Meenakshi Chakraverti,
Neal Davis, Kay Emel-Powell, Michael Ferry,
Katharine Freeman, Dean Kimmith, Linda LeClair,
Allegra Lockstadt, Matthew McGlincy, Craig Mod,
Timo Parfitt, Nolan Skochdopol, Eric Tucker,
Lani Willis, Tarn Wilson, Grant Wood,
C Pam Zhang, and many anonymous donors

Rikki Ducornet is a transdisciplinary artist. Her work is animated by an interest in nature, Eros, tyranny, and the transcendent capacities of the creative imagination. She is a poet, fiction writer, essayist, and artist, and her fiction has been translated into fifteen languages. Her art is exhibited internationally, most recently with Amnesty International's traveling exhibit *I Welcome,* focused on the refugee crisis. She has received numerous fellowships and awards, including an Arts and Letters Award from the American Academy of Arts and Letters, the Bard College Arts and Letters Award, the Prix Guerlain, a Critics' Choice Award, and the Lannan Literary Award for Fiction. Her novel *The Jade Cabinet* was a finalist for the National Book Critics Circle Award.

Trafik was designed by
Bookmobile Design & Digital Publisher Services.
Text is set in Warnock Pro.